Red Heart Tattoo

Lurlene McDaniel

Red Heart Tattoo

DELACORTE PRESS

Text copyright © 2012 by Lurlene McDaniel
Jacket art © by Plush Studios/Getty Images

Visit us on the Web! randomhouse.com/teens
Educators and librarians, for a variety of teaching tools,
visit us at randomhouse.com/teachers

Library of Congress Cataloging-in-Publication Data
McDaniel, Lurlene.
The red heart tattoo / Lurlene McDaniel. — 1st ed.
p. cm.
Summary: Tells the story of a school bombing, portraying the relationships and events leading up to the incident as well as its repercussions.
ISBN 978-0-385-73462-2 (hardcover) — ISBN 978-0-385-90461-2 (glb) — ISBN 978-0-307-97411-2 (ebook)
[1. School violence—Fiction. 2. Interpersonal relations—Fiction. 3. High schools—Fiction. 4. Schools—Fiction.] I. Title.
PZ7.M4784172 Red 2012   [Fic]—dc22   2011016584

The text of this book is set in 12.5-point Filosofia.
Book design by Vikki Sheatsley
Printed in the United States of America
10 9 8 7 6 5 4 3 2 1
First Edition

For Peg and Mary Lou

Prologue

AT 7:35 A.M., the day before Thanksgiving break was to begin, when Edison middle and high school students were congregating in the commons area before the day's classes commenced, the bomb detonated.

The explosion sent most of a cantilevered staircase crashing to the floor and smashed the short decorative wall surrounding the staircase where students sat, segregated by class status. The best and most visible places along the wall belonged to the seniors. Farther down sat the juniors, then the sophomores, until the wall was packed with the school's pecking order royalty.

The explosion happened in a nanosecond, bursting first with a brilliant flash of white, followed by a deafening roar that shook the atrium commons. Clouds of gray debris that blocked out the morning colors from the shattered skylight were flung into the air.

When the blast was over, nothing that existed before would ever be the same again for those who attended Edison.

On that morning nine people died instantly.

Fifteen were critically injured.

Twenty-two suffered less severe injuries.

And one was blinded.

Part One

September–November

1

Morgan Frierson looked across the football field, at stands filled with Edison students, all stomping and cheering for the start of the pep rally. A frenzied exhibition of school spirit would guarantee that Edison's principal and staff would authorize another such rally. And who didn't want to cut out of last period thirty minutes early? Morgan knew some kids were already melting away into the Michigan afternoon, ditching school and the rally, but most were hanging around in the stands.

She stood at the mouth of the short tunnel leading from the locker room, the football team stamping behind her, waiting for Principal Simmons to finish his comments on the makeshift stage in the middle of the field. The marching band had already played and gone through a few formations, and now its members were standing at the foot of the stage, sweating in the hot sun. Morgan fidgeted impatiently, and when she felt the brush of lips on the back of her neck, she jumped a foot.

"Whoa, babe! It's a kiss, not a knife," she heard her boyfriend, Trent Caparella, say.

Behind them, a few of the players made smacking sounds and off-color remarks.

Trent turned, saying good-naturedly, "Knock it off, dirtbags."

Morgan spun to face Trent. "You startled me."

Trent was a soccer player, but during football season Coach used Trent's kicking leg to add necessary extra points and field goals to the scoreboard. "Nervous, Madam President?"

They were seniors and Morgan had been elected student council president. Today was her first public speech to the student body. "Nervous? How could I be? I just love talking to a thousand kids who are going to ignore me."

"Never happen. When they see you coming, they'll bow."

"Very funny." Morgan chewed her bottom lip, heard her name from the principal's mike. She took a deep breath. "Here I go." She jogged onto the field, looking at the ground so she wouldn't trip. Catcalls and cheers erupted from the stands. She glanced up to see her best friend, Kelli, and a whole squad of cheerleaders waving at her. The front rows of the stands were packed with her fellow seniors, benches of honor at every pep rally, off-limits to the other kids.

Morgan trotted up the platform stairs, her hair

bobbing on her shoulders, and went to the mike. "Seniors, juniors, sophomores, freshmen!" The bleachers yipped with whistles and stomping. Each class attempted to outscreech the others. Morgan quickly decided to dump her prepared remarks about school spirit. "Here they are!" she shouted. "Your Fighting Eagles!"

The football team, dressed in bright blue-and-white uniforms, jogged out onto the field, and the students did their cheering duty, led by the cheerleading squad. Morgan kept her eyes on Trent. He was gorgeous: tall, blond, broad-shouldered, with bulging leg muscles from years of playing soccer. She felt so lucky to be his girl. Ever since their freshman year, when they'd first set eyes on each other, they'd been a couple—"the Jock and the Princess, a Disney movie in living color." That was what Kelli had always said about them. Morgan couldn't deny she agreed with her friend's analysis. She and Trent *were* a perfect couple; everyone said so. He was one of the reasons she'd been elected student council president, and they the Most Popular Twosome for the yearbook. But she'd earned Most Likely to Succeed and become a Merit Scholar on her own. No denying she was driven to earn high grades and college scholarships. Trent had already been offered athletic scholarships from top universities. They would be going their separate ways after graduation. That was hard for Morgan—knowing that this was their last year together before their lives changed forever.

The team jogged around the football field. Cheers. Kelli and the cheerleading squad flashed pom-poms, made human pyramids, executed precise tumbling routines. More cheers from the bleachers. The band struck up the school song and air horns sounded out of nowhere. The principal beamed toward the stands. Morgan felt a deep stirring of school spirit and teared up. For a moment, her gaze connected with Trent's. He blew her a kiss.

And then, without warning, in front of the goalpost at the east end of the field, all hell broke loose.

2

Firecrackers went up; bottle rockets and shrieking banshee noises exploded out of a box painted in the school colors that had been sitting innocently between the goalposts. The bleachers erupted with screams and expelled them in waves. Like rats pouring from a sinking ship, kids flowed downward, outward across the field, running in every direction. Simmons grabbed the mike from Morgan, yelled, "Stay calm! Please, don't run!"

Morgan froze, watched in horror as the cheerleaders were overrun, the band shoved aside. She lost sight of Kelli's dark hair in the melee. Above, the sky went bright with sprays of colored sparklers, a July Fourth bonanza in September.

"It's fireworks!" Simmons yelled into the mike. "That's all. Just fireworks." No one was listening.

Morgan felt someone grab her arm, turned to see Trent holding her wrist.

"Come on!" he shouted, pulling her down the platform steps. With his arm around her, they dodged fleeing students, jogged to the side of the field and into the tunnel.

She stopped, turned as the last of the noise and fireworks subsided. Pale smoke dissipated into the bright blue sky. By now the field was completely empty of human life aside from Principal Simmons, still standing on the platform and clutching the mike. The ground was littered with paper, shredded pom-poms and a few lost shoes. Morgan was trembling. "Who would do this?"

Trent shook his head. "Some jerks."

"But why?"

"Probably thought it would be funny."

"Do you think it's funny?"

He shrugged. "Maybe not funny. But it sure got noticed."

"Please don't tell me you or Mark had anything to do—"

Trent threw up his hands, backed up. "No way. We'd never pull something like that. Not our style. That prank took coordination and planning. We were in class or with the team all afternoon." He rested his arms on her shoulders, leaned his forehead against hers. "I love you, babe. I wouldn't ever rain on your parade."

She believed him. Plus, he was right. The fireworks show had been well planned and executed. Someone had wanted to ruin the pep rally—*her* pep rally, the one she'd arranged, fought for and endorsed. She felt a burning in her chest and stomach as her fear morphed into anger. "I'm going to find out who did this."

"I guess everyone wants to know." Trent stated the obvious.

Morgan stared hard at him, fire in her brain. "And when I do, I'm going to make sure they're tossed out on their butts."

Her parents were waiting for her when she walked in the front door. "Are you all right?" her mother, Paige, blurted.

"I told you I was fine on the phone." Morgan was still mad, and she hadn't expected her parents to shut down their law offices and rush home early. She'd patiently explained that the fireworks drama was a stupid prank and that no one was even near the display when it went off.

"It's all over town," said her father, Hal. "Some cellphone video clips are already up on TV. Kids took pictures while they were running away. Pretty bad video, but you get the sense of panic."

Morgan knew the clips would go viral in no time. That made her madder.

"Was anyone hurt?" Paige asked.

"Scrapes and bruises in the scramble to get away." It had taken Morgan thirty minutes to make her own getaway from school grounds and the parking lot, dodging police and firefighter response teams. Her cell had buzzed constantly during the drive home.

"Kids could have been trampled to death," her mother insisted.

"Any idea who the culprit was?" her dad asked.

"Not a clue."

"We'll make sure the book's thrown at them once you find out."

Her cell vibrated as another text came in. Morgan looked at the message. She still hadn't heard from Kelli, although she'd texted her twice. Not Kelli this time either.

Paige stepped up and hugged Morgan. "We're glad you're safe."

"Me too," Morgan mumbled, swallowing a teary lump in her throat. She wasn't sure if the lump meant relief from not being hurt or if it was from the pure fiery knot of anger she'd been nursing. Whoever had done this was going to pay.

3

He had always thought she was pretty. Probably because of her red hair and green eyes, a dynamite combo, to his way of thinking. Stuart Rothman—Roth to everyone—had studied Morgan Frierson from a distance ever since sixth grade, when he'd first landed in Edison Middle School. They were seniors now, and she was popular and well liked, with a string of wordy accomplishments attached to her name. He had a list of words after his name too—most of them negative. It didn't take a degree in rocket science to recognize that she was out of his league. Plus, she was superglued to Trent, the soccer star, a guy Roth had disliked on first sight. Why did the jocks always get the pretty girls? And why did the pretty girls flock to the jerks?

Roth blew through a yellow traffic light in the center of downtown—dead-in-the-water downtown. Grandville,

Michigan, was nowheresville to Roth, a dying town of shuttered factories that had once catered to the auto industry. Now Main Street was Dead Street, with a few businesses still hanging on, including his uncle Max's tattoo place, the Ink Spot. Roth pulled his pickup truck into one of the many open spaces near Max's shop.

He went inside, where Max was inking a fat man's shaved back. The air smelled of fresh ink and antiseptic cleaners. Max looked up, the hum of his tattoo needle pausing. He pushed his glasses up onto his forehead. The fat man never stirred, although Roth knew that inking was painful, even with numbing cream. He wore his uncle's ink art on his own body, so he knew how it felt to be tattooed. "You all right? What happened at the high school?" Max asked. "It's all over the news."

"I'm fine. Someone set off fireworks to celebrate the pep rally." Roth crossed to the minifridge and dug out an apple.

"And you know nothing about it?"

"Not a thing."

Max gave him a long, hard, skeptical look. He was a big man, a former marine with a permanent limp from an accident that had ended his military service. "No injuries?"

"A few kids got knocked around in the stampede out of the stadium."

"But not seriously?"

Roth didn't meet his uncle's gaze. He took a big bite of the apple. "That's what I heard."

"You know, if whoever did this is caught, they'll be expelled."

"I think whoever did it will be smart enough not to get caught."

"Better be." Max held Roth's gaze for a long moment, lowered his glasses and set back to work.

"Where's Carla?" Roth asked.

"Running errands. She'll head straight home and start on supper. You should go to the house too. She'll be worried about you."

"I'll go tell her I'm right as rain."

"Got homework?"

A history paper due on Monday, two workbook pages of advanced algebra and a hundred pages to read in a novel for English. "Naw. Not a lick," Roth said.

"We always had homework when I was a senior," Max said without looking up.

Roth shrugged. "Times change."

Max blew air through his lips in disbelief. "I expect you to graduate next June. It's not optional."

"Don't worry. I'll be up there ready to walk."

"Tell Carla I'll be home in an hour."

Roth finished the apple and walked outside into the crisp late afternoon. The air had turned cooler, and the oak trees along Main were tinged with color. Leaves had already fallen into the bed of Roth's older-model pickup. He liked keeping the blue truck spotless. It had been a gift from Max and Carla when he'd turned seventeen the year before, the one possession Roth counted as truly belonging to him. All the rest of his life was on loan—his home, his family.

He'd been orphaned at the age of seven, his biological

parents blown up in a meth lab cook gone bad, and had become a ward of the state. He'd passed through three foster homes by age ten. His uncle Max had stepped up and taken him when Roth was eleven and Max's military career was over. Max had no idea about raising a kid, especially an emotionally wounded one, so there had been a lot of adjusting at first, with Roth pushing every boundary, waiting for Max to get rid of him too.

Max had been hard on him, a drill sergeant who knew nothing about being a parent. Roth had no one else and he didn't want to return to foster care, so Max made a pact with him. "Look, we're family. This isn't the way it should be for either of us, but it is. Took me a while to wrestle you from the state, but here we are. We're all we got."

Max had given Roth a slice of his family history too, stuff Roth had never known. "Your dad—my bro, Jake— started on drugs in middle school. He got hooked young. Our parents sent him to rehab twice. I was older and in the military, so I missed a lot of the drama. Mom would write me about him, but there was nothing I could do."

Roth had listened closely. The father he remembered was mercurial, moody, sometimes happy, sometimes mean. Roth had steered clear of him, hiding in a closet when his dad became explosive. "And Mom?" he'd asked Max.

"Nancy was a sweet girl. No one could believe it when she married Jake. It was between rehab stints, I think. Loved him, she told me. But the drugs were too strong; he couldn't kick them. The drugs broke him in every way."

"But she helped him cook meth. She was a druggie too."

"Not for a long time. Not while she was carrying you either. She loved you, Roth. Your dad's and my parents passed within months of each other and your mom's parents were dead too. I was stationed overseas. She had no support system. Jake couldn't hold a job; they were head over heels in debt. She started using too."

Roth remembered some of this tender, nice mother, the one who had held him whenever he got hurt, hid him when Jake was acting crazy.

"They started their own meth lab to make money," Max explained. "But she always made sure you were out of the house when they cooked. That stuff . . . the chemicals . . . they wreck your brain one way or another. She would lock you in their car and park it away from the house so you wouldn't breathe the fumes."

And one night the house had exploded and all Roth could do was watch it burn to the ground. Still, hearing the story from Max had helped Roth feel he'd been loved once. So he had settled down—sort of. No drugs was the one thing they agreed upon. School attendance and good behavior, not so much. Everything had gotten easier for both of them once Carla came into Max's life, married him and moved in.

Carla was a strong, kind, well-inked woman with a smoker's voice and a soft spot for Roth. He needed that. He was haunted by the image of a fireball that lit up the yard and the house. He'd tried to get out of the car, tried to run and rescue his mother. He could do nothing. When the firefighters and police found him, he was a pale, shivering, wide-eyed kid who refused to cry.

So who was he now? A freak who pushed the edges of life's envelope, a nowhere kid—not bad, not good—wondering where he fit. Roth turned on the truck's radio, tried to find a local station that wasn't reporting on the pep rally fireworks, but couldn't. He sighed, turned off the radio and drove home.

4

"Mom, I don't want to go to the ER," Kelli Larson said. Her mother was weaving down side streets, avoiding main streets clogged with police vehicles and fire trucks and anxious parents trying to get their kids away from Edison High School.

"You fell from the top of the human pyramid, Kelli. There's no way I'm *not* taking you into the ER for X-rays." Jane Larson's look of determination was fierce.

Kelli felt a wave of panic. No way did she want to hit the ER. They might want to do blood work with her X-rays. "I fall all the time, Mom. Jennie broke my fall. She's the one who's hurt. I'll just have a few bruises."

Jane glared at Kelli. "Your wrist is swollen. It needs an X-ray."

Kelli fought to calm her breathing, racked her brain for a way to change her mother's mind. Her wrist hurt like crazy, but she refused to complain. That would just make her mother even more determined to elbow her way into the ER. "Listen," she said, with a sudden inspiration. "Take me to Dr. Trubey's office instead."

"Your pediatrician? Why go see him?"

Kelli only saw Trubey for extreme illnesses and annual checkups now that she was a senior. Teens like her were caught in a no-man's-land between child and adult doctors—too old for the former, too uncomfortable with the latter. "He has an X-ray machine. He can X-ray my wrist. I mean, can you imagine how backed up the ER is? Everybody's going there, even for a scratch. Why should we be stuck for hours waiting our turn?"

She saw her mother cut her eyes her way and realized she'd scored a point.

Kelli's heart hammered harder in her chest. Dr. Trubey was a kindly man in his late sixties who'd been her doctor since she was a newborn. He'd check her over and X-ray her wrist but wouldn't require blood work like the ER would.

Jane turned at the corner and Kelli breathed a sigh of relief. Dr. Trubey's office was divided into two waiting rooms—the sick-kid room and the well-kid room. Both were full, but Kelli took a seat in the well room. She recognized students from her school who'd had the same idea about avoiding the ER, and speculated that they all recognized her. As a cheerleader, she was seen every year in front of the football stadium bleachers, plus she was still in her uniform. Her mom went to the sign-in window and

Kelli whipped out her cell from her purse. She had nine text messages, four from Morgan.

R U OK?

Whr R U?

Call ME!

NOW!

Two were from Mark, her boyfriend.

U OK?

At hom. Txt me.

The remaining texts, from other cheerleaders checking on her, didn't matter. She'd get to them later. She put off texting Morgan and went straight to Mark's number. She wanted to talk to him, needed to hear his voice, but texting him back was all she could do for the moment. She thumbed her way through a quick return message to his cell.

Doc. Wrst x-ray. Wil cal latr.

It hurt her feelings that he hadn't added "I LV U" or any number of sweet things that he could have to his message. Hurt her a lot. She closed her cell just as her mother returned from the check-in window, and forced a smile.

Jane settled in the chair beside Kelli with a grumble. "We'll have to wait."

"Not as long as at the hospital," Kelli said brightly. Her wrist throbbed, but she didn't let on. She felt threatened from all sides—her position on the team, her relationship with Mark, her grades. No need to bring that up with her mother, but she already knew she was going to have a bad year. A very bad year.

．．．

"Well, it isn't broken," Dr. Trubey told Kelli and her mother, waving the X-ray as he came into the examination room. "A bad sprain, though. I'll wrap it and give you a sling."

Jane said, "She has a game tomorrow night."

"No games for you, little girl," Dr. Trubey said to Kelli. "Not for at least six weeks."

"Six weeks!" Jane blurted.

"She can cheer in two weeks, but no tumbling routines. She could do some real ligament damage if she injures her wrist further."

"But she's the head tumbler," Jane said. "The team looks to her."

Dr. Trubey skewered Jane with a look over the top of his glasses. "No tumbling."

Kelli wasn't as bummed about the layoff as her mother. At the moment, she hurt all over and just wanted to go home.

"She's a fast healer," Jane said.

Dr. Trubey concentrated on the wrap. "Sprains take time to heal. Don't push it."

Kelli was grateful for his intervention. He understood Jane Larson well.

Her mother watched, hawklike, while Dr. Trubey wrapped Kelli's wrist in gauze and Ace bandages. He sent them off with care instructions, a prescription for pain medication and a wave of his hand. It was after seven when Kelli eased back into the car. They hit the drive-through at the pharmacy, waited for the pills. Kelli swallowed two as soon as she could. "Why don't we grab a pizza and take it home," Jane said.

Her offer surprised Kelli. Her mother watched both of their weights vigilantly, so she almost never suggested pizza. "You must really feel sorry for me," Kelli said.

"Of course I feel sorry for you. You're hurt."

And as a result, Kelli thought, she might lose her position on the squad. And Kelli knew how important the cheerleading squad was to her mother. Jane had been a cheerleader herself at Edison years before, and Kelli often thought she would still have liked to be one. High school—Jane's glory days. "Pizza sounds good," she said.

There was no one waiting for them at home. Her parents had divorced when Kelli was a freshman, and her dad had moved to New York. She missed him. Her mother was a real estate agent, but the market was dead everywhere, so she was home more than usual and very discontented with life.

"You'll be back on top in no time," Jane said, reaching across the console and squeezing Kelli's good hand. Jane laughed. "Get it? On top?"

"I get it, Mom," Kelli said wearily. Kelli was the smallest person on the squad and always topped the human pyramid. It was one of the reasons Jane fussed at Kelli about weight control. Fat girls didn't climb to the top.

"I hope they catch the little perverts who did this," Jane said. "You have any idea who it might have been?"

"No idea." Kelli leaned her aching head against the car's headrest as the pills began to work and made her mellow. Still, she wanted to get home and talk to Mark. Her world—*their* world—was upside down and she needed him more than anything.

5

Morgan moved the food around on her plate, anxious to get dinner over with and go up to her room. She was too wired on adrenaline to be hungry. Her parents sat at the table with her, none of them interested in food, it seemed. Her father had turned off all cell phones and put the home phone on the answering machine. Because the Friersons were two of only five attorneys in Grandville, their phones had rung continuously all evening. Morgan had listened to Paige and Hal tell callers, "It's too soon to think about litigation, Mrs. So-and-so," and, "We can't blame the school just yet, Mr. Whatever-the-name."

Morgan speared a lima bean and asked, "So what happens now?"

"The police will question people."

"The police!"

"In this era of homeland security, explosions are taken seriously."

"It was fireworks," Morgan insisted.

"They didn't combust without help." Paige inserted her opinion. "Someone set them up and set them off. It was planned."

Morgan was still angry at the person or persons who had done it, but she wasn't crazy about the police sniffing around. She wanted to find the culprits and throttle them. She had developed a plan for the school year, ideas and directions for her student council term—good ideas for projects and fund-raising. Now some idiot had interjected himself into the mix, and not in a good way. Her brain hurt from thinking about it. She'd dig around on Monday. Someone knew something.

"Could this have been the work of a rival school?" her father asked.

Their closest rival was Bonnerville, thirty miles away. "Pranks are usually reserved for the last week of classes," Morgan said, "so it's unlikely."

"The football team?" Paige offered.

"They didn't do it. They wouldn't have," Morgan snapped.

"I'm just asking. So will the cops."

Hal, seated at the head of the table with his wife and daughter on either side of him, put his hands on both their shoulders as if separating warring factions. "I only hope it doesn't scrap the season." The game endorsed by the pep rally had been postponed "until further notice."

Morgan hadn't considered that. Trent needed this season as a kicker; all the senior players did, because college scouts hung around the games in the fall looking for talent. "They won't dare scrap it."

Hal shrugged.

"Did you hear from Kelli?" Paige changed the subject quickly—a lawyer's trick.

"She sent me a text. Sprained wrist. She'll be all right." Morgan would have driven right over, but since the next day was Saturday and Kelli had said she just wanted to crash, Morgan would go over in the morning.

"Stupid prank," Paige muttered.

They finished the meal in silence.

One o'clock in the morning and Morgan was wide awake. She sat cross-legged on her bed surfing the Web on her laptop. She had her parents' trust when it came to using the Web, and she was a girl who, as Kelli said, "colored inside the lines." Morgan worked hard not to lose that trust. Plus, Morgan was pretty sure her mother checked the laptop's cache memory from time to time, so Morgan stuck to a couple of parent-approved social websites and sites that could support a claim of "homework research." She did, however, have her email password protected along with a software program that deterred hacking just in case Mom decided to dig, which Paige swore she'd never do. The safety locks were for the sake of her and Trent's privacy. They sent some pretty racy emails to each other and no way did she want her parents reading them.

The house lay quiet, so when Morgan heard the sound of sand splattering against her bedroom window, she looked up instantly. The sound repeated. She quickly unfolded herself and hurried to her window. Sure enough, she saw Trent staring up at her from below. He waved. She held up her hand, motioned that she'd be down, slid on her fleece-lined slipper boots and stole from her room, down the hallway, past her sleeping parents' room and down the stairs.

In the foyer, she grabbed a lightweight coat from the closet to cover her pj's and eased out the door into the chilly night air. Trent met her on the porch, put his arms around her and kissed her forehead. "What's up?" she asked.

"Wanted to see my girl."

"I wanted to see you too." She hugged him hard and they kissed. Her knees went weak. The leather and wool of his letter jacket scraped her chin when she drew a breath.

His hands slipped inside her coat and beneath her flannel top. She shivered. His hands were cold, her skin warm, and her every cell was suddenly awake at his touch. "Let's go to our tree," she whispered.

They crossed the front lawn to the giant maple in the middle of the acre-sized yard—Trent called it their "meet-and-greet tree," a place where they had privacy, thanks to the low-hanging branches. "I'm going to miss these leaves when they drop," he said into her hair.

"I learned how to cut leaves out of construction paper in kindergarten. Maybe I can make some and glue them on."

She felt him smile. "You're so smart."

"Not smart enough to figure out who played that stupid prank today."

"Yeah . . . the team's hopping mad. Coach ain't too happy either."

"We'll get another shot at them," she said, deciding not to mention the possibility her father had raised about a canceled season.

Trent kissed her again. He pushed his back into the trunk of the tree, pulled her against the length of him. She clung to him, her insides going gooey. He must have felt her eagerness through her clothes, because he whispered, "Wow. I didn't know you came alive after midnight."

"No way you could. It's after my curfew," she mumbled, letting his hands rub beneath her pajama top.

"Remind me to sneak up to your room next time."

She pulled back, suddenly realizing she didn't want to lose her virginity under the maple tree in her front yard. He relaxed his hold on her, saying, "Sorry. You just turn me on. I love you so much."

"Same for me," she said, breathing in a gulp of fresh cold air. They had so far kept their pact to stay within certain physical boundaries with each other. It was difficult, but neither wanted to change the directions of their plans for themselves—college with scholarships.

They rested their foreheads together, breathed slowly in unison, regaining control. "I better go," Trent said.

"Good idea."

He walked Morgan to her front door. She eased inside,

but before pulling the door shut she said, "We need to figure out who ruined our pep rally."

"I'll poke around. You know how rumors fly. Anyone who pulled this off probably can't help bragging about it."

"I've been looking on the Web," she said. "So far nothing."

"I have the gift of persuasion on my side." He balled his hands into fists.

"No pounding," Morgan said. "Promise me."

"No pounding," Trent said.

But it was too dark for her to see if his fingers were crossed when he said it.

6

The Watchers stood against the wall of the atrium on Monday morning . . . watching. The area was thick with bodies, swarms of students standing, sitting, talking, eating, clustering in groups of belonging. The edges of each group didn't touch. Unwritten rules of high school. No mixing. No touching. No mingling. If you were in the atrium before first bell, you were in a group. You were a part of something. No standing room for loners, for those who were different, who didn't fit in.

The Watchers had found each other in seventh grade because they never belonged to any group. Their very separateness made them a group of two automatically.

"What did you think of Friday's pep rally?" the taller, thiner one asked.

"Hysterical," the shorter, heavier one said, taking a bite of a toaster pastry. "Wish we'd thought of it."

"The whole school's talking about it."

"Might be cool to have the whole school talking about something we did." The pastry eater wiped away fallen crumbs. "In a neat way, of course. You know, admiration."

"You think?" the thin one said.

"Sure. Wouldn't you like to be the ones they're talking about? Sort of our secret. 'I know something you don't know.'"

The thin one rocked back against the wall. "The fireworks were clever, but not genius. Can't imagine any of them smart enough to think of it." The thin one gestured toward the mass of students. "Look at them. A bunch of stupid cows."

In unison their gazes shot to the low wall where the most popular of the popular were gathered, the seniors, the beautiful ones who everyone knew and wanted to be like, even the social rejects. The outcasts never verbalized their yearnings, but the Watchers knew it to be true. It was written on the faces of the others, in looks of either downright envy or disdain. Everyone knew who the best of Edison were. No secrets about that.

"I hate them," the short one said. "Every stupid one of them."

"How much?"

"What do you mean?"

"How much do you hate them?"

"I don't know. A lot."

"Enough to do something about it?"

The short one stopped chewing the pastry. "Like what? What are you thinking?"

32

"Do you really think you could stomach something more than a toaster pastry when it comes to doing something to them?"

The heavyset one turned red, embarrassed by the tone of derision in the other's voice. "I told you I hate them just like you do."

"Maybe I should think of something to get everyone talking."

"I'm listening. What are you thinking of doing?"

"I don't know. Yet." The tall one smiled coldly.

"You'll tell me when you think of it?"

"It'll be better than fireworks, that's a promise."

"And we'll do it together?"

"You'll be the first to know. We're friends, aren't we?"

The short one felt relieved to be back in good graces. The thin one was mercurial, quick to verbally torture, just as quick to change direction and focus. Sometimes impossible to read.

Just then first bell rang and the groups began to spread out before the tardy bell rang. "Look at them. They're like cockroaches." The thin one shoved away from the wall. "See you after school. We'll talk more."

"About . . . ?"

The thin one grinned. "Immortality."

They sauntered to classes down separate halls.

7

"Why do you do that?"

"Do what?" Roth turned toward the girl who'd just walked up.

"Stare at that conceited Morgan."

They were in the cafeteria on Monday. Roth was slouched in a metal chair, a palm-size electronic video game—strictly forbidden on school grounds—in his hands and the black hood of his sweatshirt pulled over his head. "Well, just say what you think, Liza," he retorted.

Liza Sandiski sat down with a clunk in the chair next to his. "Well, it's true," she said huffily.

Roth and Liza had been friends for years. They were both outsiders. Her short, spiky hair was cut asymmetrically and dyed coal-black with purple tips. She wore studs in her nose and tongue and a line of small silver hoops the length of one ear. She sported a small star, inked by Roth's uncle Max, on her right cheek, just under her eye. None of her other tats showed, but Roth knew where each one was located on her body because he had explored it thoroughly. "Bad weekend?" he asked.

She shot him a mean look. "Don't change the subject. Why do you keep sneaking peeks at Morgan? Or is it her boyfriend who turns you on?"

Roth saw Mr. Champs casing the cafeteria for behavior problems and contraband, so he shoved his video game into the kangaroo pocket of his sweatshirt. "Now you're just being snarky," he told Liza. "Trent's a total jerk. Morgan's just pretty. Easy on the eyes, and I like her long legs." He knew he was being hateful to Liza, who had body issues. She was short, heavier than she wanted to be, always railing against skinny models in magazines or movie and TV stars showing off bony arms and legs. He'd tried many times to make Liza feel better about herself, but it was a losing battle. He saw her stiffen, felt bad about his comment, put out his hand and held her wrist. "My bad."

She glared at him.

"Truth is, I'm casing Morgan's table for signs of them knowing anything about last Friday."

Liza's gaze shifted to the senior table filled with Edison elites—Morgan, Trent, Kelli, Mark, the cheerleading squad—all of the people she disliked by sight. "The pep rally?"

Roth grinned.

"The fireworks." Liza's eyes widened. "It was *you*!"

"You might not want to shout that out."

"No way!"

"Way."

Liza smiled, her whole face softening. "You turd."

"Yeah . . . ain't I a stinker."

"When did you set it up?"

"Four in the morning. I figured no one would check a cardboard box painted with school colors lying on the field under the goalpost. And I was right."

"But how—?"

"Secret's all mine." Roth thought she looked skeptical, as if she didn't quite believe him and thought he was taking credit for someone else's prank. "I did it," he insisted.

"You should have told me. I would have helped."

"This needed to be on me if I got caught."

"Where'd you get the fireworks?" Still skeptical.

"Bought over July Fourth."

"You've been planning it since July?"

Roth shrugged. "Not sure when the idea came to me. It just did."

"Why?"

"Why not? Thought it would be fun to shake up the new student council administration, I guess."

Liza's eyes narrowed and she homed in on Roth's face. "So it still comes back to Morgan, doesn't it?" She stood, scooting back her chair, making it scrape the floor. "You need to get another hobby, Roth. She'd never be interested in a guy like you."

Liza stalked off. Her words cut him like a knife, not because they were cold and hurled like stones, but because they were true.

• • •

"I don't like the way that guy keeps looking at you," Trent said into Morgan's ear as he leaned down and kissed her neck.

"Don't do that. Champs is on the prowl," she said, embarrassed. "What guy?"

"That creep over there. Tattoo guy." Trent nodded toward a corner of the room where only a few kids sat alone gobbling lunch or reading a book.

Her gaze darted up and instantly connected with Roth's. Her cheeks burned because his look was raw, intense and unreadable. She quickly glanced away. It wasn't as if she hadn't seen him staring at her before. What was worse, her heart thudded and her pulse raced whenever she caught him watching her. There was a tingle that came with it, a thrill she was drawn to in spite of loving Trent. She felt like a traitor.

"Just sit here with me," she told Trent. "Ignore him."

"I want to knock his face in."

"Why?"

"Principle."

"Stop it," she said with a smile. "Looking's harmless." From the corner of her eye, she saw Roth get up and leave the cafeteria by a side door. She felt relieved—not because Roth irritated Trent, but because his presence distracted her.

"Thought I'd come over after football practice," Trent said. "Hang out. If that's okay."

"I have a council meeting until four-thirty. Then I'm

supposed to meet Mom at the Sub Shop. Dinner," she said. "Dad's working late."

Trent groaned. "I can't come by after midnight all the time just to see you."

Morgan saw heads lift all around them. She elbowed Trent in the side. "One time," she corrected.

He grinned, waggled his eyebrows. "But it was a very good visit."

Her friends made mocking tsk-tsk noises.

Morgan squared her chin, glanced around at the group. "All right, everyone. Show's over. Get back to work."

They laughed. Everyone except Kelli. She barely mustered a smile. Morgan thought Kelli hadn't been very sociable on Saturday morning either. She'd chalked it up to the pain her friend was experiencing. Now she wasn't so sure. Come to think of it, Mark wasn't his usual jovial self either. A fight? Usually Kelli spilled her guts to Morgan whenever she and Mark had it out.

Morgan made a mental note to corner her best friend and make her tell what was going on. Then she remembered all the stuff she had to do—classes, meeting, dinner, homework. She'd text her, although she was sure Kelli wouldn't confess anything in a return text message. Morgan sighed and picked up her tray. There were just too many things going on in her life right now. How was she going to juggle it all and keep track of Kelli's boyfriend problems too?

The bell rang, so Morgan hustled to class.

8

"She cut you? She can't cut you! That's just wrong. Who does Linda Holland think she is?" Kelli's mom raged. They stood in their kitchen, where Kelli had just told Jane about her last class of the day and a meeting with her phys ed teacher.

"She's the coach, Mom," Kelli answered wearily. She'd hoped her mother wouldn't explode when she told her the news about being cut from the squad, but obviously it had been wishful thinking. "And she didn't cut me. She benched me. She needs someone who can perform and be tossed around. I can't." She held up her wrapped sprained wrist to make her point.

"Well, we'll just see about that!" Jane fumbled for her cell.

"Mom, please! It's all right. I'm not upset because I got benched."

"Well, I am."

Kelli wanted to shout, *It's not your life,* but she didn't. In truth, Jane had never embraced that almost twenty years had passed since she'd attended Edison High School and been voted most popular and been a queen bee, dating Brock Larson, the football team's quarterback. Kelli snatched Jane's cell phone away. "Don't call her. Please!"

"What's wrong with you? You love performing on that squad."

"Not right now. Classes are hard this year. I don't mind stepping back."

Jane crossed her arms, fumed. "Who got your slot?"

"Elana Mendez."

"That Mexican—"

"She's good, Mom," Kelli interrupted.

"You beat her out last spring for the position, so she wasn't as good as you."

"She deserves my place now."

"What about when your wrist heals? Is Linda going to give you your spot again?"

"Football season will be all but over in six weeks. Doc said it would take—"

Jane scoffed. "And in January basketball starts. Then soccer. You don't have to lose the entire year. You need assurances that this Mendez girl will be out once you heal. She's a junior. She'll have another year to be on the squad after you graduate in June."

If *I graduate,* Kelli thought. She felt as if she were

talking to a stone wall. Why didn't her mother get it? Kelli didn't *want* her place back on the squad. She was through with being a cheerleader. Finished with the acrobatics, the falls, the bruises, the constant weight watching. There was so much that her mother didn't understand and that she couldn't explain at this moment.

Jane's features softened. "Believe me, honey. These are the best years of your life—"

"Give it up, Mom. You've told me this a thousand times."

"Don't raise your voice to me. It's the truth. Before you know it you'll be out here in the real world grubbing for a living."

Like me . . . The unsaid but implied words hung in the air. Kelli put her hands over her ears. "Not now, Mom. Just give it a rest! I don't care about cheerleading. I don't care that Elana got my place. I. Don't. Care."

Kelli turned and ran from the room while her mother stood speechless.

Morgan sat with a sobbing Kelli in Kelli's wrecked bedroom, trying to comfort her. "Do you really not care about losing your slot to Elana, or is that just something you told your mother?"

Kelli blew her nose. "I really don't care."

Morgan hadn't expected that answer. The cheerleading and dance squad had meant everything to Kelli since ninth grade. "Then if it doesn't matter, why are you crying?"

41

Kelli picked at the fringe on a pillow, stared down at her hands. "It's just—it's just everything."

"You and Mark?" Morgan ventured her best guess. "You two have a fight?"

Kelli nodded, wiped her eyes. "I'm afraid he's dumping me."

"Impossible! You two are like spaghetti and meatballs. Ice cream and cake—"

"Oil and water," Kelli interrupted.

Usually Kelli ran to Morgan with details of every word that passed between her and Mark, but she had been pretty withdrawn lately. "Why do you think that?"

"He never calls anymore."

"Well, with football practice and classes—"

"Last year he texted me five times a day. All summer we went places together."

"I know. Trent and I were with you."

"Now I have to practically trip him in the hall to get his attention."

Morgan was baffled. How could she have not noticed? "So you think he's into another girl?"

"Girls flirt with him all the time."

"But you don't know that for sure."

"I don't know anything for sure."

"Well, then—"

"Don't." Kelli held up her hand. "I don't want to talk about it right now."

Morgan sat, still puzzling over her friend's behavior. "You have been kind of moody lately. Guys don't like moody, you know." Trent liked Morgan happy and honestly didn't know how to handle the days when she felt controlled by her hormones. She didn't know how to handle such days either, so she kept to herself when they happened.

Kelli sprang off the bed. "Don't you start on me!"

"I'm not." Morgan glanced around the bedroom heaped with clothes and old food wrappers, unwashed plates and glasses hardened with milk stains. "I've—uh—never seen you let your space get so trashed before."

"Well, thanks, *Mom*," Kelli snapped. She scooted off the bed and started picking up the mess on the floor.

"Hey, I didn't mean—"

"Just go," Kelli said, a sharp edge to her voice.

Offended, Morgan recoiled.

Kelli marched to her closet, dropped a pile of wadded clothes onto the floor and hung her head. "I'm sorry. I didn't mean to be ugly to you. I'm just trying to figure out some things. Forgive me?"

Morgan stood up. "Of course. I—I hate to see you so unhappy. We're friends. We should be able to talk about what's bothering you."

Kelli clutched a jacket to her chest, a jacket Morgan recognized as one of Mark's. "I will," she said. "I just need some space right now."

"I can live with that," Morgan said, not certain she could, but knowing she shouldn't pressure Kelli. Nobody liked to be nagged. Kelli would talk to her when she was ready. She walked to the door, paused. "You're my best friend in the whole world, Kelli Larson. I don't think it's right to let Mark make you crazy. I know he loves you."

"Right," Kelli mumbled without conviction. "He just doesn't love me enough."

Baffled and confused, Morgan left Kelli alone in the ruins of her bedroom.

9

"Carla, you here?" Roth called out as he walked through Uncle Max's house. He heaved his book bag onto the counter and looked at the kitchen clock. It was after five.

"You by yourself?" Carla's voice answered from the back porch.

Roth opened the door and stepped onto the weathered wood deck. Carla sat in an old lawn chair. She was wrapped in a quilt, one hand hidden from sight. Roth winked. "Just me."

She blew out a mouthful of smoke and eased her hand forward to reveal a cigarette. "Good," she said. "I just lit up and would have hated to toss it."

Max didn't like her smoking and she'd tried to quit many times, but every now and then she slipped up and just had to have one. Roth was the only person who knew. She slid a lawn chair toward him with her foot. "Sit."

45

Roth flopped.

"He called to say he was running late, so I took a chance. Don't ever start smoking, then you'll never have to stop." She took a long drag. "How was your day?"

"Before or after Trent Caparella and his jock buddies got in my face?"

"Why'd they go after you?"

"Trent doesn't like me looking at his girl."

"Is she pretty?"

Roth flashed a devilish grin. "Best-looking girl in the school."

Carla laughed. "You touch her?"

"Not yet."

"She worth getting beat up for?"

Roth shrugged. "Haven't decided."

Carla searched him with her eyes. "Sure you have."

"Never could fool you," he said with a laugh.

Carla was more a mother to Roth than his real one had been so many years ago. His memory of both his parents was sketchy; the thing most vivid, most haunting in his memory was the ball of fire that had taken them away. He kept a wedding photo of them in the drawer beside his bed. Max had given it to him. "You should remember them when they were happy," Max had said. "Not what they became after meth took them over." Roth had been angry at his parents for years, all the time he had spent in foster care, before Max had come along, war-wounded but determined to raise his brother's kid. Why had his parents loved meth more than him? He was their flesh and

46

blood. Meth was just in their blood. And yet meth had won the war for their minds and bodies. Roth was collateral damage.

"Just be careful," Carla said, snuffing out her cigarette and standing. "Don't let some jealous boyfriend work you over."

Roth knew that was how Carla had come into Max's life. A jealous boyfriend had been beating her up when Max stepped in and evened the odds. Six months later, she'd moved in with Max, and two months after that, they married.

"I'll be careful," Roth said, knowing full well that he wouldn't. If he decided he wanted Morgan, he'd go after her full throttle. This was his last chance. They'd be graduating—well, she would. He'd never see her again. To hell with the consequences.

Morgan was called to the principal's office the next morning. Her nerves tingled. Being called into Mr. Simmons's office was usually not a good thing. She smoothed her hair, sucked up her courage and marched down the hall. When she arrived, Principal Simmons introduced her to two detectives from the Grandville Police Department. "Detective Wolcheski." The short round man nodded. "And Detective Sanchez." The dark-haired woman smiled.

"We want to ask a few questions about the fireworks last Friday," Wolcheski said.

Morgan remembered that her parents had told her not

to be questioned unless they were present, so she said, "I'll call my parents."

"Why?"

Simmons jumped in with "The Friersons are attorneys. They're just uptown."

"Do you really think you need a lawyer to answer a few questions, Miss Frierson?" Sanchez asked.

Morgan's heart pounded. "Mom said to call. . . ."

Wolcheski rolled his eyes.

Principal Simmons made the phone call.

Paige and Hal were there in twenty minutes. Once Morgan and her parents were seated in the cramped office, Paige asked, "What questions do you want to ask our daughter?"

The detectives stood beside the desk looking down at them like birds of prey to Morgan's way of thinking.

Sanchez said, "Mr. Simmons tells us she was the person who organized the pep rally. Is that true?"

To Morgan's ears, it sounded accusatory, like she'd planned everything that had happened—the good *and* the bad.

Hal nodded at Morgan. She could answer. "The student council planned the rally."

"And you're the president?" Sanchez asked.

"I am."

"What did you plan?"

"To pump up school spirit before our game that night. The marching band was to play special music; the cheerleaders were to perform some cheers and gymnastic routines. Mr. Simmons approved everything."

"And the fireworks?"

"Not part of our plan."

"So whose plan was it?"

"Now, come on," Hal interrupted. "You can't possibly think the student council sanctioned a secret fireworks display."

Wolcheski turned toward Hal. "Here's what I know, Mr. Frierson. The fire department and the police department turned out in force, at great expense to the taxpayer, for what turned out to be a prank. We're trying to find the culprit and maybe seek reimbursement for time and personnel costs from the responsible party or parties."

"The fireworks came as a total surprise to all of us," Morgan offered.

Detective Sanchez crossed her arms, leaned against the principal's desk and looked hard into Morgan's eyes. "You know, when I was in high school, there was always someone, or a group of someones, who ran the place. A queen bee, a gossipmonger, someone who knew everything that went on within our hallowed halls. I have no reason to believe that's changed in today's high schools. Kids talk. Kids know."

Morgan felt her face grow hot with temper. The woman was practically calling her a liar. "Well, no one's talked to me, Detective. I'd like to find out who did it too. It spoiled the pep rally and made our team miss a game."

A long, awkward silence stretched, until Hal said, "I think this interview is over. My daughter knows nothing about this incident. If she did she'd tell you." He stood. "Now if you'll excuse us . . ." He took Morgan's elbow.

49

She glared at the police but stepped to her father's side.

"If you hear anything," Sanchez called, "you will contact us, won't you, Miss Frierson?" She held out a business card. Paige took it.

Once in the hallway, Morgan said, "They think I had something to do with it. They think I'm lying."

"They're fishing," Hal said. "Using intimidation. Ignore them."

Morgan was so angry she was shaking. "I don't know anything!" However, she did know that it would be all over school that she'd been called to Simmons's office and questioned by the police. That should make whoever had set off the fireworks feel very satisfied and safe.

"Calm down," Paige said. "We may never know who did it, so don't worry about it. It's over."

"Over? I don't think so. We'll never have another pep rally. Whoever did this will get off scot-free."

The bell rang. Classroom doors banged open and kids flowed into the hall. "We'll talk at home tonight," Paige said above the din of chatter and shuffling feet.

Morgan said, "I've got to hurry. I don't want to be late for next period."

"See you at the house," Paige called as Morgan hurried away.

Morgan seethed all the way to class. She knew the police didn't believe her. That message about a "queen bee" was a dead giveaway. That was what she was to Detective Sanchez—a privileged brat who knew more than she was telling. *I don't know who did it, but I will.* Whoever did this wasn't going to get away with it.

10

"So did the cops frisk you? I would have," Trent joked.

"Not funny. They think I'm involved," Morgan said. They were standing beside the staircase in the atrium after school. The herd of students leaving had thinned, but the area was still noisy with echoes of voices and foot traffic. Trent was heading to the gym for football practice, but she'd stopped him to unload her story about her police interview.

"Babe, cops always think everybody is guilty. It's what makes them cops."

"I just wish . . . I mean, if you could have seen the way that woman detective looked at me. And our principal didn't stick up for me!"

Trent kissed her forehead. "Let it go. Besides, I think I have something interesting to tell you."

"Like what?"

His brown eyes went mischievous. "No info without a tongue kiss."

Her cheeks warmed. "Trent . . . we're in the middle of the hall."

"And?"

She glanced around. No one was paying any mind to them, but still she was uncomfortable. PDAs—public displays of affection—weren't her style. Alone with Trent under their special tree in her front yard was more to her liking. "Later," she said.

"Can I stop over after practice?"

Her parents would be working late, but they didn't like her having Trent over when they weren't home. "Fifteen minutes. And only outside."

"Wow. Clampdown." He didn't look happy about the conditions.

"You can't focus on fifteen minutes of me and you under the tree?" She poked him in the chest with her finger. Truthfully, it was getting more difficult to be alone with him—somehow their clothes kept falling off. They'd gotten dangerously close to "doing the deed" more than once.

Trent shrugged grudgingly. "I guess I'll have to."

She dipped her head to catch his gaze. "A really good fifteen. Now, what news do you have for me?"

"Heard some whispers about the fireworks. Roth's name got mentioned."

Her heart tripped. "Rothman?"

"Yeah, tattoo boy. Locker-room talk. Could be true. Nobody likes him."

Morgan pressed her lips together. Rumors often held a grain of truth. "Why?"

"Why not? He's got a rep for trouble—King of Detention Hall, Most Likely to Be Sent to the Principal's Office. He could have his own bad-rap page in the yearbook."

"How am I going to find out?" she said, mostly to herself.

"I could beat it out of him."

She flashed him an exasperated look. "My problem. I'll handle it."

"Be careful. He's not a nice guy. Look, I got to go. Coach hates us being late."

"See you later," she called as he jogged off.

He turned, pedaled backward. "Count on it."

Morgan sat on the half wall near the staircase to think. *Roth.* The boy with the full sensitive lips and startling blue eyes. The boy who made her pulse go crazy and her palms sweat when he stared at her. She was pathetic. Suddenly his attention toward her made sense—he was probably watching her for a reason. But why? What had she ever done to tee him off enough to make him pull such a prank?

The image of his goth friend, Liza Sandiski, flashed through Morgan's mind. Grunge-looking Liza with so much hardware in her face that she'd set off metal detectors. She and Morgan once had a run-in, during last year's student council campaign. Morgan had bravely (to her way of thinking) approached the group of goth girls in the halls to pass out her "Vote for Morgan" literature. Liza had taken the flyer, stepped closer and torn it into small pieces

53

right in Morgan's face. "I'm not voting," Liza had said. "No one running I like."

Everyone had laughed and sauntered away while Morgan stood feeling humiliated. Had Liza put Roth up to the fireworks prank? And if Liza had asked, would he have done it? Morgan grew agitated. If it was true, she wanted to know. Hadn't she sworn not to let the perpetrators get away with it? She grabbed her book bag and made a dash for the parking lot. She needed to get started on homework before Trent arrived. And if Trent's report was true, she needed to figure out how to best handle Roth and maybe Liza too.

Kelli sat cross-legged on the gym bleachers, staring at a history book but waiting for the football team to come through the doors from the locker room. Practice was over, so they had to come out this way once they showered and changed. They had to pass through the gym to get out of school and into the parking lot. Sooner or later, Mark had to come out where she could talk to him.

Three weeks had passed since she'd been hurt, and she had yet to pin him down for a serious talk. Her texts went mostly unanswered, or minimally answered, things like "GOT 2 RUN" or "PLEZ NOT NOW." If she caught him in the halls, it was the same story. If she called his cell, he didn't pick up. Today was the day she was determined to corner him. She was desperate.

The locker-room doors slammed open and the team poured out, talking, laughing. Kelli looked up, waiting until the flow turned into a trickle. For a moment she thought he'd known she was waiting and had slipped away. But the stragglers came out, among them Trent and Mark. Kelli shot off the bleachers and rushed up to Mark, saying, "We need to talk."

He gave her a deer-in-the-headlights look. "Uh—I can't now."

"Yes, you can," Kelli said. "You owe me."

Mark glanced at Trent, who shrugged. "I'll wait in the car."

He must have driven them both to school today.

"Wait—"

"Now," Kelli insisted.

Mark got a defeated hangdog look and nodded. He followed her to the hard wooden bleachers, sat gingerly, stared at the floor.

"Why are you avoiding me? You know what's happening."

"I'm not avoiding you. It's just that we already talked this out. I won't change my mind."

Tears of frustration sprang to Kelli's eyes. "You can't do this to me! It's not fair."

He looked up, his expression tortured. "I know. I'm a jerk. But you know how I feel, Kelli. I've wanted to play ball all my life, ever since Pop Warner. I'm good. Coach has college coaches calling about me. A full ride, Kelli, at almost any university in the Midwest. My folks can't send me to college. Dad hasn't worked steady in two years. This is my chance."

"And what about my chances?" she cried. Tears were streaming down her cheeks now. "What about *me*, Mark?" She held up her still-splinted wrist. "This is going to heal. Then what am I going to tell my mother?"

"I never wanted you to get hurt—"

"Save it. You're killing me," she said through clenched teeth.

He reached out to touch her, but she scooted out of his reach. "I—I love you."

"Don't even say that to me. I hate you."

His face went pale and his eyes misted, but he stood quickly. "My offer still stands, Kelli."

"Your offer." She said the words as if they tasted bitter. "It wasn't an offer, Mark. It was an ultimatum."

He stood over her for a few seconds, lifted his book bag from the floor and walked away.

Kelli wept for a long time, alone in the tomblike quiet of the gym after the door clicked closed behind him.

11

The Watchers stood in their usual places in the atrium, leaning against a wall near the bathroom door, out of the stream of foot traffic, and observing the cliques of Edison, the hoods of their heavy sweatshirts raised to hide their faces.

"You said you had a plan?" the short one asked the tall one.

"It's bold. You may want to chicken out when you hear it."

"I won't! I keep telling you I'm up for whatever you're planning."

"Once you know my plan, there's no turning back."

"Why do you doubt me? We're friends, right?"

The thin one jammed hands into pockets. October's cold air seeped through the cement walls. The school administrators were too cheap to pay to heat the atrium, so everyone shivered. On the half wall next to the staircase, Morgan sat wrapped in Trent's letter jacket, laughing at a joke someone had told. The tall one found their esteemed council president especially irksome.

"Know what I heard?" the short one asked.

"Will I care?"

Undaunted, the other one said, "I heard that Roth set the fireworks."

The tall one turned full attention on the short one. "Where'd you hear that?"

Waves of satisfaction washed over the short one. The great smart one hadn't heard the rumor. This was a coup. "Around. Sounds like something he'd do, though." A glowering dark look crossed the tall one's face and brought satisfaction to the one who'd shared the rumor.

"So Roth is a badass. So what? What I've got planned will make his joke look stupid."

"I said I wanted to know your big plan."

"*Our,*" the tall one said. "We're doing this together."

"Okay."

"You have to come over to my house. I'll show you everything on my computer."

"You could email it to me."

The tall one glared down at the other. "My plan can't be spread from computer to computer. I know how to eradicate all traces on my computer. You don't."

The heavy kid bristled but knew the assessment was correct. Smart, yes. Supersmart, no—not smart like the other one. "When should I come over?"

"This afternoon. I'll be the only one home."

"How am I supposed to get there?"

"You walk, flabo. It'll do you good."

The short Watcher's face burned with shame. In his gut he longed to be defensive or to say something back. But he knew better. The other Watcher was in charge, and that was the way it would stay. At least there was someone to call.

The bedroom was like a cave. The walls were painted black, with black lights in two lamps and a lava lamp on the dresser. Gaming posters of death and destruction, of war and carnage hung on the walls, slapped up haphazardly. The rumpled bed was wrapped in black sheets that glowed purple under the black lights.

"How do you see in here?" the short one blurted.

For once, the smart one seemed oblivious. A laptop, two backup hard drives and a lamp with a halogen bulb sat on a desk. "When you're in my room, call me by my Web avatar name. It's Apocalypse."

"Really? That's cool. Who can I be?" The short one regretted the question as it came out.

Apocalypse smirked and said, "How about Pop-Tart, since you like them so much."

"I don't think I like—"

"Or Pop-Fart. Your choice."

"Please don't make fun of me. It—it hurts my feelings."

"So I'll call you Executioner. That better?"

"Yes. Much better."

Apocalypse shrugged, fingers flying over the laptop keys. After several screens of bland, boring websites, an encrypted file was found and loaded. It popped open and caused Executioner's breath to catch. "Is that . . . is that a diagram of a *bomb*?"

"A thing of beauty, yes?"

"You're going to build a *bomb*?" Executioner asked, voice trembling.

"*We're* going to build a bomb," Apocalypse said. "Together."

"But, I don't know how to build—"

"I have instructions."

"But a bomb . . ."

"Not a huge one. Just something to make noise, mess up the atrium. You said you wanted people talking about us."

"But how will they know it's us? I don't want anyone to know—"

"Man, you're dense. No one will know it's us but us. It'll be talked about forever. Isn't that what we want? Fireworks are nothing. But a bomb—no one will ever forget that."

"What if someone gets hurt?"

"So what? You're such an idiot. We don't care about those people."

Executioner was flabbergasted, but the idea wasn't a total turnoff either, not after one of the jocks had "accidentally" doused Executioner with chocolate milk earlier in the week.

"But the stuff to build it . . . ?"

"I have a list. We'll buy it a little at a time. Use cash. We can work in my garage, behind that pile of junk in the corner. No one will ever know."

Executioner stared hard into Apocalypse's cold blue eyes. "You're—you're serious, aren't you?"

"Serious as a heart attack. I will do this. *We* will, 'cause now you're in."

Morgan was steaming mad. The school halls were empty, the bus carrying the football team to the away game and the caravan of students' cars following the bus were gone, and here she was stuck putting up posters for next week's homecoming bash by herself. Where were the rest of her council and helpers? They had said they'd stay behind and help, but instead everyone had made a dash to leave as soon as the bell buzzed. Everyone, of course, except Morgan. Now she'd have to drive to the game alone, *after* she hung all the posters.

She told herself to be grateful that they still had a football season to play after the fireworks stunt over six weeks before. The season had teetered on disaster for twelve days, but Coach, the players and their parents had rallied to save the season for the sake of the boys being scouted by college coaches. Mr. Simmons had also gone to bat for Edison, pleading before the school board that one bad apple shouldn't ruin it for everyone.

Morgan kept telling herself "Be grateful" as she hurried to staple posters on school-authorized corkboards when she heard a noise. Someone came up from behind, placed hands firmly on either side of her shoulders, trapping her in between. She yelped in surprise, spun and, with her back pressed against the wall, found herself staring into Roth's electric-blue eyes.

Her heart hammered and a ribbon of fear skidded down her spine. "What do you want?"

"I hear you're gunning for me," he said.

"I don't know what you're talking about." She looked right and left, but the halls held no one else and were silent as a tomb.

"You're asking questions. Spreading rumors."

"What if I am? Asking questions, I mean. What rumors am I spreading?"

"You're saying I did the fireworks stunt. Why are you telling people that?"

"It's what I heard. I want it confirmed."

"Why didn't you come to me and ask?"

Her heart slowed and her fear morphed into anger. "Like you would have told me the truth."

"You'll never know now, will you?" He was leaning in toward her. His peppermint-candy breath felt warm on her cheeks. "The fireworks business is old news. Give it a rest."

"Digging up dirt takes time."

He searched her face, managed a beguiling smile. "And you don't have anything better to do than dig around in old dirt?"

She knew with the next beat of her heart that he

absolutely had pulled the prank. She pressed hard into the wall to put space between them. Her pulse was racing. "I don't think what you did was funny. And I can still report you." If her threat bothered him, he didn't let it show.

"So now you're judge and jury? You say I'm guilty, so I am? Where's your proof?"

He had her there. She had no real proof, just rumors. "Your stunt was a bad joke. And in case you missed it, no one laughed."

"So what does make you laugh, Morgan Frierson?" He leaned so close that his full mouth hovered inches from her own. His hair was damp, as if he'd just come from the gym showers.

An emotion unrelated to anger or fear shot through her, making her knees go weak. She said, "Back off."

Slowly he straightened, dropped his arms loosely to his sides, flashed a smile. "I don't want a fight with you, Morgan. Can't we agree to forget ancient history?"

She glanced downward, not wanting to meet his eyes. She let out a breath and fought to regain her composure. At the moment a vendetta against him seemed futile and childish. Too much time had elapsed. What was she going to do, rat to the principal and the cops at this late date? "If anything like that happens again, I will nail you to a wall."

Looking unruffled by her threat, he inclined his head graciously. "I accept your terms."

His cavalier attitude only made her angry again. "Go away," she said.

He glanced down at the posters she'd dropped when

he'd captured her. He bent to pick them up. "Want me to help you put up the rest of these?"

"I don't need your help."

"Well, I asked," he said, shrugging. "I volunteered to help my president. Put it in the record." He stepped backward. "Later," he said.

Never, she thought.

As he handed her the posters, she saw that his black hoodie was only partially zipped. No shirt beneath it. On the area between his collarbones, she read a single word tattooed in blue ink into his skin.

Wicked.

12

Roth banged on Liza's front door.

She opened the door, looked surprised to see him.

"You going to invite me in?"

He looked cross. She stepped aside, letting him pass. Her home was in its usual state of disarray. Both her parents worked and neither one seemed to care about housework, at least not to the naked eye. "My room," she said, leading him to a familiar destination. Her room was in no better shape than the rest of the house. The bed was littered with abandoned clothes. Roth sat on the floor, his back braced by the bed.

He hadn't been around in weeks and Liza had missed him. She settled cross-legged in front of him. "So what's up?"

"Had a run-in with our school president on Friday. She was putting up homecoming posters."

Liza's radar went up. "How nice for you. Did it make your day?"

"Not so nice," he said.

"Are you asking me to the big dance?" Sarcasm dripped from her voice.

"You know I don't go for that crap."

"And yet you've mentioned it to little ol' me."

"Knock it off, Liza. I mentioned it because Morgan and I had a little talk."

Liza raised her knees, locked her arms around them. "Again, how nice for you."

Roth ignored her sour tone. "She accused me of the fireworks prank. Said she heard a rumor about me doing it."

"So?"

"So you were the only person I told. How did she hear about it?"

Liza's face reddened. "I have no idea."

He leaned forward. "Come on. You had to have been the source."

She shrugged, capitulated. "Sue me."

"Why?" he asked. "Why did you say anything to anyone? It was my secret and I shared it with you only. Nobody else had a clue it was me."

"People suspected. You've got a rep for doing stuff," she said defensively.

"Suspecting and knowing are two different things. What if she tells her jock friends? Or goes to Simmons? Or the police?"

Liza hadn't thought about that. She'd just been pissed off at him, jealous that he was so caught up in Morgan that day in the cafeteria. He wanted Morgan, an overachiever who got everything she ever wanted while girls like Liza got nothing. Liza had seen it coming for over a year in the way Roth cast covert glances at the red-haired girl when he thought no one was watching. Roth and Liza had been friends since sixth grade, when he'd been a scared, rebellious kid, lashing out at the world. She understood him, accepted him without judging him. He was the only boy who'd ever paid her any attention and she'd given herself to him completely. She'd thought they would be together always. But lately she'd felt him pulling away.

"Why, Liza?" Roth pushed her to confess.

Liza stood, walked to the window and fiddled with the wand on the blinds, fought off tears. The late-afternoon sun made slat marks across her body. "I didn't mean to out you. I was just talking with one of my friends and . . . and it slipped out. I told her to keep it to herself."

"But she didn't."

"I'm sorry, okay?" She turned to face him. She looked contrite. "I never thought it would go so far. I thought everyone would forget about it after a few days."

Silence descended. Roth stared up at the ceiling.

Liza asked, "Do you think Morgan will blab?"

He shrugged. "Who knows? But she's got something on me, and I don't like that hanging over my head. I promised Max I'd graduate. I won't if I'm expelled."

"I could talk to her—"

"No. Stay away from her," he commanded.

Liza stiffened, stung by the sharpness in his voice. "You can't tell me what to do."

"I can when it comes to me and my business. I trusted you, Liza."

Liza shut the blinds, darkening the room. "It's Morgan, isn't it? You've got a thing for her, haven't you?" Painful as she knew it would be, she wanted to hear him say it.

Roth stood up. "I said what I came to say."

She wanted to hurt him like he was hurting her. "She already has a boyfriend. She won't give you the time of day. Look at you . . . with your tats and studs and attitude. You're a loser to a princess like her."

He started for the door. Liza realized she'd gone too far, said words she couldn't take back. She hurried and grabbed his elbow. "Hey, don't go. I'm sorry about every-thing." Desperate to keep him from walking away, she slid her gaze to the rumpled bed. "My parents won't be home for hours. I can prove to you how sorry I am. Stay with me."

Roth heard the invitation but broke free of her grip. "I trusted you. You blew it. Now stay out of my life, Liza. I mean it."

"Don't punish me," she cried. "Don't leave."

Without a backward glance, he closed the door behind him. Liza stood stunned. She had lost him in the way she wanted him most, as his girl. Roth was through with her. His excuse of betrayal was just that—an excuse. He wanted what he wanted. And it wasn't Liza.

• • •

"You two look awesome!" Her mother snapped yet another picture of Morgan and Trent.

Morgan rolled her eyes. "Mom, I think we have enough photos on the memory card to qualify you for Paparazzo of the Year."

"Your mother's right," her father said. "You'll be the best-looking couple at the dance."

"Just one more," Paige said, reaiming her camera. "I have the homecoming queen and king standing in my living room. You bet I'm going to record the event for posterity."

Morgan and Trent had been crowned the night before, during halftime of the football game. Tonight the dance was being held in the school gym. Morgan had spent the day decorating the space, then stopped at the beauty salon. The stylist did her hair in a sophisticated French twist with long springy tendrils surrounding her face. The upsweep would show off her glittering crystal earrings. Her dress bared her shoulders and was a deep, vibrant green that set off her pale skin.

Trent, who was wearing a dress jacket and blue jeans, looped his arm around Morgan's waist and said, "Okay, one more." He leaned in and mugged for the camera and Paige pushed the button.

"Oh, that's a good one. I'll put it on Facebook."

Morgan shook her head impatiently. By the time she and Trent were out the door, the sun was setting. "We're going to be late."

69

"Not with me driving." They were almost to the car when Trent pulled her short. "Wait a minute."

"We need to go now—"

"I want to give you something first. They can start the dance without us."

She snapped his letter jacket under her chin against the October chill and let him pull her toward their special tree. The leaves shimmered with fall colors against a sky that gleamed with a rising harvest moon. Once under the tree he pulled her into his arms and kissed her. Her heart thumped eagerly, as it always did when Trent held her. "*That's* worth being late for," she said in his ear.

He laced the fingers of his left hand with hers. His face looked sweet and serious, part small boy, part grown man. "Hope this is too," he said. He reached into his pocket, withdrew a small box.

Morgan's eyes widened. "What's this?"

"Open it."

She eased off the lid, saw a ring nestled on top of a wad of cotton. Her gaze flew to his face.

"A promise ring," Trent said. "I promise to replace this one with an engagement ring one day."

She just stared at the ring, set with a single glowing white pearl. "We—we have college—"

"I know that," he said, plucking the ring from the box. "But when college is over, we'll come home and we'll have forever. I'll never love anyone like I love you."

Forever. With Trent. Morgan couldn't take a breath. Her mind whirled. She'd been so caught up in the here and now, with her grades and homecoming and college applications, she hadn't thought about "forever."

"You like it, don't you?" His face clouded. Her heart swelled with tenderness and tears misted her eyes.

"It's beautiful. I love it."

"And you'll wear it?"

"Yes."

A grin broke across his face. He fisted the air. "Yes!"

She laughed, let him slip the ring onto her shaking hand. She was reeling, heady from the intoxication of the moment. She threw her arms around his neck. "I love you so much."

"Now we can go to the dance," he said. "I want to show you off."

Laughing, holding hands, they ran to the car and chased the moon all the way to the gym.

13

Morgan's big disappointment at the homecoming dance was that Kelli didn't show up. Even as late as yesterday, Kelli had told Morgan she was coming. They'd talked about makeup and hair and which shoes would look best with Kelli's pink off-the-shoulder dress. Yet when Morgan and Trent arrived and caught up with their group of friends inside the gym, Kelli wasn't with them.

Morgan went straight to Mark. "Where's Kelli?"

"She didn't want to come."

"Since when?"

"Since September."

His words took Morgan by surprise. "She said the two of you were coming together. She told me so."

Mark jammed his hands into his pockets. "Then she lied. She never planned on coming. At least not with me."

Incredulous, Morgan got the bottom-line message.

Kelli had *lied* to her—to Morgan, her supposed best friend! "Why?" she asked. "What's going on between you two?"

Mark's jaw tightened. "Nothing. It's over between us."

"Since when?"

"For a while now."

Morgan felt like an idiot. Why was she hearing this from Mark and not Kelli? She recalled Kelli crying on the phone and saying that Mark had someone else, another girl. Was that true? "So who did you bring?"

"I came alone. Be sure and tell her that."

Morgan had a million questions, but just then Trent slipped his arms around her from behind, nuzzled her neck. "Am I going to have to spend the night refereeing you two?"

"Game over," Mark said, walking away.

"Wait!" Morgan called. Mark kept moving. She turned to Trent. "Do you know what's happening with them? Kelli won't tell me anything. She lied to me about being here tonight."

Trent threw up his hands. "Don't want to know."

"But—"

He dipped his head and kissed her, stopping her words. From the corner of her eye, Morgan saw two chaperones eyeball them. She ducked. "Let's not get thrown out."

Trent led her to the dance floor. "Then let's not talk about Kelli and Mark. This is our night, not theirs." He took her into his arms while lights from an overhead

73

spinning machine threw a sea of sparkle and color over the dancers flowing around them.

One of the cheerleaders spotted Morgan's ring and shrieked. Girls clustered like a bouquet of spring flowers to admire the pearl. "Engaged?" one girl asked.

"Promise ring," Morgan said. "College first."

"Boy, I wouldn't let him get far away from me," another girl said. "Why risk him getting picked off by some babe?"

Morgan felt self-conscious about the attention they were giving the ring. Sure, she loved Trent, had loved him for almost three years. And yet the promise ring represented a commitment that she found strangely unsettling. What if she didn't want to get married right after college?

Trent broke into the circle. "Hey, babe. Me and some of the guys are going out to the parking lot for a minute."

Code for "Having a smoke and a sip of something eighty-proof." Her stomach knotted. "What if you're caught?"

"Won't be. We're going way off campus. To the mall parking lot." The mall was half a mile away. "We'll be back in a while."

She wished he wouldn't leave, but she knew it was a male ritual she couldn't fight. "What if they check your breath when you come back in?" The chaperones were hugging the doors, their eyes darting everywhere suspiciously.

"Gum and mints. A guy's best friend," Trent said.

Morgan watched Trent and his buddies slip away, staggering their exits so as not to be noticed. She sighed, feeling deserted. She missed Kelli. If her friend had been here, they would have hunkered down and commented on every girl and dress in the gym. But there was no Kelli. And to compound her absence was Morgan's knowledge that Kelli had told her a bald-faced lie.

All of a sudden the air seemed stale. Morgan eased over to the table where she and Trent had placed their belongings. She picked up Trent's letter jacket and headed toward the bathroom, slipping on the wool-and-leather coat emblazoned with the letter *E* as she walked, nodding to Mrs. DeHaven as she passed through the door into the hall. She paused at a side exit door, looked both ways, saw no one watching her. She eased outside into the cold night air, which stung her lungs but also felt refreshing after the closed air of the gym, thick with scents of perfume and hair spray and perspiring bodies.

Morgan needed to think. She needed to figure out what was going on with her feelings. Why had Kelli not come to her with the truth about her and Mark? Morgan had sensed something was wrong between the two of them, yet she hadn't pushed Kelli for answers. What kind of a friend let something as important as a breakup get past her without pressing for answers? Morgan felt guilty.

The moon was overhead now, brilliant and bright. She walked slowly, deep in thought, and ended up at the football field. The carpet of grass looked blue in the moon's white light; the bleachers were slivers of silver, the goalposts glowing rods rising out of the ground. She walked onto the field, her heels slipping in the manicured grass.

Her shoes would be a mess, but at the moment she didn't care. If it were warmer, she'd take off her shoes and feel the sharpness of the turf on her bare feet.

She stopped in the center of the field, stretched out her arms and lifted her face to the moon. Its light had swallowed the dimmer light of distant stars. Her mind tumbled over thoughts like water over stones—Kelli, their friendship, the promise ring, her college dreams, her future with Trent. She held out her arms like a worshipper, letting the moonlight wash over her. She closed her eyes, hoping to wash away the jumble of confusion rolling through her.

She stopped when she heard somebody clapping over near the bleachers. Her eyes popped open and she saw Roth coming toward her across the field, dressed in black—boots, jeans, hoodie. "What are you doing out here?" she asked, shocked by his sudden brooding appearance. She wasn't afraid of him. She felt infringed upon, but not afraid. He stopped in front of her, his hands shoved into the kangaroo pocket of his sweatshirt.

"Watching you in the moonlight."

A preposterous answer, but still it made her pulse quicken. "Did you come to the dance?"

"I don't dance."

"And yet you're here."

"Nothing else to do tonight." He tipped his head to one side, pulled the hood off his head. His rumpled hair made him look darkly sexy. "So what brings you outside?"

She owed him no explanations, but she wondered as much herself. Had she somehow sensed his presence?

"Fresh air. Trent went off with his friends, but he'll be back soon."

Roth grinned. "Is that a warning for me to get lost?"

"It's a free country." His emergence from the bleachers disconcerted her. In the moonlight, he made her feel off balance, out of kilter. She didn't understand why he had this effect on her, especially when she was in love with Trent. And yet he did. Roth seemed edged with danger, forbidden and, therefore, compelling in her well-thought-out and ordered world.

He touched her crystal earring, made it swing. "You look pretty."

She swallowed, unable to take her gaze from his face.

"Your hair's up. It's pretty, but I like it better down." He took his hand from her earring to behind her head and touched the twisted hair, sending chills up her spine. "May I?" he asked.

Morgan could scarcely breathe. Her body felt lighter than smoke and about as substantial. And despite the trip to the salon, the hour enduring a beautician messing with her hair until her scalp hurt, plus endless squirts of hair spray, she nodded.

It took him only minutes to pull out the hairpins, un-twist the knot of her hair, fluff it all around her shoulders. He dropped the pins onto the grass. "That's better," he said.

She shook her hair, untangled it with her fingers. He helped by dragging his fingers behind hers, which caused her heart to thud harder.

Inevitably his fingers touched the ring. He caught her

hand, held it up and studied the ring. He rubbed the pearl with his thumb and watched it glow. "He has good taste in all things."

Agitated, unnerved, feeling unsure and misplaced in this new universe of confused and clashing emotions, she whispered, "I—I love Trent."

He stared down at her for a long time, holding her in place with a look she couldn't read but couldn't break free of either. "Then why are you out here with me and he's nowhere around? I would never have left you alone."

She had no answers for him. Her teeth began to chatter. "I—I'm cold."

"Then you'd better go back inside while you can."

She didn't need another prompt. Morgan turned and hustled off the field as quickly as her troublesome heels would allow her. Like a jackrabbit chased by a wolf, she moved toward the hulking form of the gym and to the safety of feelings she could control.

"Hey, I've been looking for you," Trent said when she hurried into the gym. The heated air felt stifling after the chill of the night.

"Went for air," she said breathlessly.

"Your cheeks are red."

"Cold outside." She smelled beer mingled with spearmint gum on his breath.

"And your hair's down. Why'd you take it down?"

"All those bobby pins were giving me a headache." She'd never lied to him, had never had any reason to lie to him, and suddenly she felt guilty, ashamed for lying now. She slid out of his jacket, hung it on the back of a chair.

"Aw . . . too bad," Trent said, looking disappointed. He rolled a long tendril of her hair between his forefinger and thumb. "I really, really like it up, babe."

"I'll remember that," she said brightly, but what she felt was the weight of Roth's fingers undoing her hair in the moonlight.

14

"I've picked D-day," Apocalypse said.

Executioner's stomach did a somersault. "D-day?"

"Stop looking so stupid. Detonation day. I told you last week, everything was ready to assemble."

They were standing in the atrium, their backs to a wall, watching the before-school foot traffic gather at the wall.

"Right . . . I just didn't think . . . you know, it would be so soon."

"Sooner the better. Come over on Saturday. My parents will be out all day."

Executioner swallowed hard. "All right." Voices echoed off the concrete walls. A high laugh from the seniors on the wall broke through the din. Both glanced over.

"They really annoy me," Apocalypse said.

"Yeah, me too." Executioner bit a chunk from a strawberry toaster pastry and crumbs scattered on the floor. "So what day have you picked?"

"Next Wednesday morning."

The last day of classes before Thanksgiving break. "That's . . . really . . . soon. . . ." Executioner's appetite vanished.

"I figured it'll give the janitors a few days to clean up the mess before we start classes again."

"How—um—how much of a mess will there be?" Executioner was foggy on the particulars because Apocalypse had said that all bombs were not created equal. Some had more bang, held more destruction than others.

"Enough to cause a nice explosion. Flash, noise—bomb stuff. Sort of like a hand grenade, but on a timer."

"So where you going to plant it?"

"I'm not sure yet, but we may not want to meet up in the atrium. And bring an old backpack when you show up on Saturday."

Executioner blinked, heart accelerating. "I'll be there." Executioner shifted from foot to foot. "Too bad no one will know it's us."

"We'll know."

"I'm just saying—"

"Well, shut up. No one can ever know. Got that?" Apocalypse drove a finger hard into Executioner's chest.

"Well, yeah, sure. I'll never say anything. You know me. I was just wishing."

"Two things." Apocalypse made a fist, ticked off points on two fingers. "Credit will never be ours. And we're not going down with the ship like those Columbine dudes. We just walk away. Because I'm smart about this and because we can."

．．．

The Wednesday before break, Morgan sat on the half wall in the atrium listening to the chatter all around her. Trent, sitting beside her, was arguing with his friends about upcoming Thanksgiving football games, potential winners and losers, and the girls, mostly cheerleaders, were gossiping. She only half heard both groups, instead mulling over her visit to Kelli's that past weekend. Kelli wouldn't even come to the door. Her mother, Jane, had let Morgan into the foyer and said, "Kelli's sick."

"She is?"

Jane looked pale, her expression strained. "Terrible case of the flu."

She had the flu last week, Morgan had thought, but she'd been too polite to say it out loud. "She's been sick a lot," Morgan said.

"Yes. That's true."

Morgan had seen Kelli at school the Monday after the homecoming dance. She'd looked awful: her hair needed to be cut and she looked frumpy tucked into an oversize sweatshirt and baggy pants. Morgan wanted to yell at her. She wanted answers about why Kelli had lied about coming to the dance, why she'd not bothered to mention breaking up with Mark. But Kelli's physical appearance made her take a different tact. Morgan had pasted a smile on her face. "You want to come over after school? We haven't hung around at my place for a long time."

"Can't. Big test tomorrow."

Morgan didn't believe Kelli. She reached out and took her friend's hand. "Please tell me what's going on. I know something's wrong. I know about you and Mark breaking up too."

Big tears filled Kelli's eyes. She squared her shoulders. "Isn't that enough?"

"It's not worth you falling apart. Not worth you giving up on life."

"What would you know?" Kelli snapped at her like a dog backed into a corner. "Your life is perfect. You live in wonderland."

Morgan dropped Kelli's hand, ripped not so much by her words but by the hot tone of her voice. "Hey, I just want to help."

"You can't help. No one can help. Just leave me alone!"

And Kelli had taken off while Morgan watched, dumbfounded. So she gave herself and Kelli some more time and on Saturday had gone over to Kelli's house only to be stonewalled by Jane. "I just want to talk to her. I know something's wrong. We . . . we were friends." She used the past tense, hoping her plea would be heard.

"And if you go upstairs and get the flu your mother will kill me," Jane said. "Call Kelli."

"She won't take my calls."

Jane pinched the bridge of her nose, closed her eyes. "Morgan, please don't push us. Just for now, go home. I'll talk to her on your behalf."

A partial admission that something was wrong, terribly wrong, with Kelli.

Morgan said, "You're scaring me. What's wrong with her?"

"Let's get through Thanksgiving, all right? Then I'll make sure she talks to you."

Morgan had left reluctantly, but she couldn't stop thinking about Kelli. Nor could she stop thinking about Roth. Ever since the homecoming dance, she'd stayed clear of him. If she caught him looking at her, she'd break eye contact instantly. She didn't want to be reminded of the things he'd made her feel in the moonlight. Roth had no place in her life. He was growing bolder, though, watching her as if he could see straight into her head. If Trent noticed, she knew he'd make Roth pay. Still, she found herself glancing around the atrium from time to time, searching for him and the tingle of excitement he stirred within her. This morning, he wasn't around.

"Babe, you want to do that with us?"

Trent's voice jerked Morgan into the present. "Do what?"

He looked exasperated. "Flag football in the park, noon on Friday, day after Thanksgiving."

She looked around. Kids were looking back at her expectantly. "Um . . . sure. That'll be fun."

"Welcome back to earth!" Trent laughed and gave her a bear hug. She snuggled against his warm body. The atrium was so blasted cold that not even his letter jacket and the sweater she wore beneath could keep the chill out. She was looking over his shoulder, at the stairwell under the cantilevered cement stairs, when she saw the blue-and-black backpack half hidden by the plastic plants. Who'd lost a backpack? And how did they lose it in such an out-of-the-way place?

She stared. "Why's that backpack in the plants?" she asked.

Trent glanced over his shoulder.

Suddenly, with no warning, a white light erupted from the dusty foliage, a light so bright, so intense that Morgan had no time to blink. A roaring sound followed, a sound like thunder, that rumbled and shook the concrete wall. She had the sensation of falling and heard noises.

And the world went dark.

Part Two

November—June

15

Roth was running to school from where he'd had to park, swearing under his breath with every step. He wasn't going to beat the bell. And he'd been doing so well with following school rules lately. He was trying, *really* trying, to keep his record clean in order to graduate. To do so meant making a supreme effort to keep up his grades and stay out of trouble for the next seven months.

The reason he was late didn't matter to the front office. And it was their fault anyway. The admin people had locked the student parking-lot gate before first bell rang. The second bell meant *you're tardy.* Today he'd had to hunt for a place for his truck and had ended up blocks away in a residential area already packed with homeowners' cars.

He had almost reached the brick steps of the main entrance when a blast knocked him backward. He staggered, crouched and covered his head as glass showered down from the atrium skylight high above. Chunks of concrete shot through the doorway. Screams erupted. The front door flew open and kids began to pour outside in a stampede, almost running him over. Some were cut and bleeding. Most were crying, shrieking. From inside the building, a low rumble shook the air. An ominous roar all but blotted out the cries and screams. Roth grabbed one kid, yelled, "What happened?"

The boy's eyes were wide and he looked shocked. "I don't know! Let me go!" He wrestled out of Roth's grip and continued running.

Roth swayed, looked up at the building, seeing not only the school but also his parents' house from when he'd been seven. Except this time he wasn't locked in a car. A cloud of concrete dust blew out of the open doors and the hole in the skylight. Roth heard kids sobbing and begging for help from inside. He elbowed his way forward, avoiding collisions with runners, hurtled up the steps and into the maelstrom.

"Holy crap!" Executioner said.

"Awesome, huh?" Apocalypse said, looking smug and satisfied. They stood, in a crowd of students across the street, watching the front of the school and the continuing stream of fleeing students. "Like rats leaving a sinking ship."

They'd stood together across the street since early morning in the cold, eyeing the school, pacing nervously, anticipating the event. "I want a bird's-eye view," Apocalypse had said. "I want to watch the lid blow off."

Executioner had agreed. No need to be any closer. What if the bomb was more powerful than they'd planned? No sense being in harm's way.

The explosion had been a spectacular sight and sound—a flash of white light followed by a boom, like a jet breaking the sound barrier. Glass had spewed from the skylight, volcanolike, and rained in glittering chunks onto the steps and sidewalk below. There had been smoke and dust and debris, but no spreading fire. The percussion explosives were more for the sake of blast damage. Apocalypse had chosen them well.

All around them groups had gathered. Many kids were cut and bleeding. Some cried hysterically. Girls clung to each other, tears streaking cement-dusted faces. Across the street, concrete dust continued to rain from the doorways and through the hole in the roof. Apocalypse turned a deaf ear to the wailing and sobbing. Executioner felt the students' pain more keenly but refused to give in to regret.

"We did *that*?" Executioner said, staring at the ruined front of the school.

Apocalypse grabbed the other's arm, dragged Executioner to the fringe of the milling crowd. "Keep your mouth shut! What if someone overhears you?"

"Ow! You're hurting me."

"If you don't keep a lid on it, I'll do worse than hurt you—I'll kill you!"

• • •

Inside the atrium Roth saw hunks of concrete strewn around the floor. He also saw bodies, heard moans. His stomach went queasy. He cupped his hand over his mouth because the gray dust and smoke were making it difficult to breathe and to see clearly. Remembering that Carla had forced a muffler into his jacket pocket that morning, Roth pulled it out and quickly wrapped it around his head, covering his nose and mouth. He stooped and kept close to the ground. His foot hit a body. He bent, grabbed the boy under his arms and dragged him into the safety of the nearest hallway, away from the worst of the carnage. He had no idea if the kid was dead or alive.

He went back into the rubble and dragged out a girl, positioning her beside the boy. The atrium grew cold from the wide-open doorways, but sweat swam on Roth's forehead, down his back and underarms. He pulled several more kids into the hall, felt his muscles twitch and strain with overexertion. *Can't stop now,* he told himself.

Still crouching, he made his way around a large hunk of concrete, stepped on something soft, recoiled. Under his feet lay Mr. Adams, a history teacher. The man's body was doughy, and blood oozed from his half-crushed head. Roth thought he might throw up, and swallowed down bile. In the distance, sirens wailed. Roth pleaded for them to hurry. He felt as if he'd been here an hour, alone with dead and dying people.

The most damage seemed to be near the staircase, so that was where Roth went. He waved his hand through the chalky air, trying to clear his line of vision, climbed over the remnants of the half wall and lowered himself onto another mound of rubble. This area was eerier, silent. He heard an ominous creak above him, looked up to see what remained of the staircase hanging by twisted cables and threads of destroyed concrete. It was going to fall.

Roth eased backward in retreat, looked down. That was when he saw a spill of reddish hair under nearby rubble. The hair was thick with dust, almost unrecognizable, but he knew whose it was. *Morgan!* Throwing away all caution, Roth leaped forward. Frantically he began to dig through the mass of bricks, tossing them behind him in heaps. Of course she would have been sitting on the wall. She always sat on the atrium wall with her group of friends before school. Today would have been no different.

His hands were cut and bleeding, but he hardly noticed. What remained of the staircase groaned under its weight. He gritted his teeth through the pain, freed Morgan's arms and pulled with all his strength. He felt her body give toward him. Something was pinning her, so he tried again. "Come on, baby," he said. "Just a little farther."

She was unresponsive. Maybe dead. He couldn't tell. He only knew he had to get her out. If she was alive and her spine was damaged, he could be sentencing her to life as a paraplegic by moving her, yet somehow that seemed better than her being crushed beneath the remains of the staircase.

Behind him, he heard voices, men and women arriving on the scene: rescuers, EMTs, police. "Over here!" he yelled. "She's trapped!"

Feet clambered over piles of brick and concrete. Roth put his arms around Morgan's chest. He gave one final tug, made one more superhuman effort, grunting with the strain, and felt her slide free. As he hauled her out of the way, what was left of the stairs gave a great shudder and fell with a roar, spraying clouds of dust and destruction in every direction. Roth threw himself over Morgan, shielding her from pelting hunks of stone and debris that hit his back and shoulders in a hailstorm of choking ruin.

"Kid! Buddy . . . you can let go now. You okay?"

Roth heard voices above him, felt hands gently pulling him away from Morgan. His muffler was gone, lost as he'd worked Morgan's body free, and concrete dust filled his mouth and nose. He coughed violently. An EMT eased him backward. Roth managed to gasp out, "Okay. I'm okay."

"Let's get you outside."

"Help her."

"We've got it from here."

Roth allowed himself to be put on a stretcher. "Is she . . . is she . . . ?" He couldn't get the question out, terrified of the answer.

He watched a paramedic place his fingers against the side of Morgan's neck, feeling for signs of life. The medic looked toward his crew and Roth. "I've got a pulse! Hey, Elroy, over here!"

Roth closed his eyes, allowed himself to be carried out into the sunlight, into the fresh air and away from the arena of death that only hours before had been his high school.

16

Chaos ruled Grandville Hospital's emergency-room waiting area. The space was packed with people, all somehow connected to Edison—parents, grandparents, aunts, uncles, brothers and sisters, teachers' husbands and wives sat in chairs or on the floor, or paced inside and outside. They talked on cell phones, cried, and shouted at staff for updates and information about their loved ones. Overwhelmed hospital personnel were patiently going from person to person, taking down data to try to connect the victims behind the closed double doors of triage, too badly hurt to speak for themselves, with frantic family members.

Among the families stuck in the ER were the walking wounded, those who had been hurt, but not so seriously they couldn't wait to be attended to. They'd been transported by overtaxed ambulances, cars and, finally, a school bus that had been pressed into service. Roth had come with the bus group because he was mobile and had been able to recite his name and address when asked. Now, sitting amid the confusion and noise, he was numb with physical pain and mental trauma. All he thought about was Morgan's limp body and the sound of the staircase's remains giving way, landing on the place where she'd lain under the rubble. The scene played on a loop in his head, each time with a violent ending of her being crushed, of her life being smashed out of her by the falling concrete.

Carla sat on one side of Roth, and Max on the other, both holding one of his gauze-bandaged hands gingerly in theirs. Blood seeped through the bandages and from scrapes and abrasions on his face and forehead. Roth ached all over. His hands hurt really bad, but he had taken nothing for the pain, although Carla had tried to force aspirin on him. He was going to wait his turn. He was going to be patient. He was hoping to hear news—any news—about others who'd been brought in.

"You need to see a doctor," Carla said, blotting the cuts on Roth's throbbing head with a clean towel.

"They'll get to him," Max said grimly. "A lot of kids hurt worse." He stared at the mass of people filling the room. "Place looks like a frigging war zone. What the hell happened? I heard there was an explosion. What exploded?"

Roth said he didn't know. Secretly he had suspicions. Not much that could explode in the atrium unless someone *wanted* something to explode. From the corner of his eye, he saw both uniformed and plainclothes cops at the doors. Several men and women were discreetly making the rounds of the people in the waiting room with small notebooks in hand.

He was staring at the floor when he heard a woman's voice above him. "Are you Stuart Rothman?"

Startled, he looked up. He recognized the imprint of Morgan's face on the woman, although she was blond, not red-haired. "Roth," he said. "Everyone calls me Roth."

"I'm Paige Frierson, Morgan's mother. One of the EMTs said you pulled my daughter to safety."

His insides went watery. "Is she going to be all right?"

"She's still unconscious. Her father's with her in radiology waiting for a CT scan."

"But she's—she's going to be okay?" he asked hopefully.

Paige's eyes filled with tears. "She's a fighter by nature."

Roth knew this to be true.

Max stood awkwardly, wobbling slightly on his bad leg. "I'm Roth's uncle and this is my wife, Carla." Carla nodded solemnly.

"Roth's a hero," Paige said. "He pulled several kids to safety. You should be very proud of him."

Max glanced at him and Roth went hot all over, feeling like a microscope specimen. "I was running late," he said. "I'm not a hero."

Max half laughed. "I guess that was a good thing today of all days."

Carla patted his arm. "You risked your life for others. That's the definition of a hero."

"Thank you," Paige said. "There aren't words to tell you how grateful we are."

Roth smiled feebly. "What was left of the staircase would have fallen on her. I couldn't let that happen."

"I'll let her know when she wakes up."

Paige was stepping away when another woman came up to Roth. She was short, had thick black hair and was dressed in a white shirt and black slacks, a police shield displayed prominently on her waistband. "Are you Stuart Rothman?"

Roth's pulse picked up. Looking at the police shield made him nervous. He didn't like cops and cops didn't like him—his tattoos and ear studs always marked him as potential trouble to them. "Yes," he said. Not wanting to be on more familiar terms with the woman, he didn't add, *Call me Roth.*

"Detective Sanchez," she said, flipping open her notebook. A man joined her. "My partner, Detective Wolcheski." The heavyset man nodded. Sanchez said, "Reports say that while everyone was running out of the school after the explosion, you ran in. True?"

"Yes," Roth said suspiciously.

"Brave thing," Wolcheski said.

"Why did you do that?" Sanchez asked.

"I—I don't know. Kids were screaming. I knew they were hurt. Thought I could help."

"And you did help," Wolcheski said. "EMTs said you pulled five kids to safety."

"I wasn't counting."

"You know anything that might help us figure out what happened?"

"I don't know what happened. I was late for classes. I was at the front steps when there was a loud boom and then everybody was screaming and running out of the building."

"Don't you know what happened?" Max asked. "You're the cops. Haven't you got a clue yet?"

The two detectives looked at each other. "Who are you?" Sanchez asked.

"Max Rothman, his uncle. His legal guardian."

"Looks as if someone set off a bomb," Sanchez said.

"A bomb!" Carla said, putting her hand to her throat. "Who'd do such a thing?"

"That's what we're trying to figure out."

Wolcheski looked back down at Roth. "You have any thoughts about who it could be?"

"No."

"But you ran inside while everyone else was running away."

"What's wrong with doing that?"

The two detectives looked at each other. "Do you know that sometimes people who create disasters play the hero afterward?" Sanchez said to Wolcheski. "They wreak havoc, then waltz in and save the day."

Max, who'd resumed his seat, shot out of his chair again, his face red and angry. "Now, you two wait a minute! Are you accusing my nephew of causing this disaster?"

"Not at all," Sanchez said innocently. "We're just saying—"

"Where do you get off saying such a thing to Roth?"

Sanchez threw up her hands. "No harm meant. Just an observation from FBI profilers. We want to get whoever did this."

Roth felt sick to his stomach, scared. All the air seemed to have left the crowded room, and the noise became a drone, like buzzing bees around a hive. Were the cops looking to blame him? He'd had nothing to do with what had happened. He was a bystander, a kid in the right place at the wrong time.

Suddenly Paige Frierson swooped back into the mix. "Excuse me. I couldn't help but overhear the conversation." All eyes turned toward her.

"And you are?"

"Paige Frierson. I'm an attorney." She turned toward Max. "Do you need an attorney, Mr. Rothman? Because I'm a very good attorney and very savvy in juvenile-law matters."

"Do we?" Max asked the two cops.

"Your call," Sanchez said, her brown eyes looking hard as steel.

Max studied the cops for a minute before nodding. "Maybe we do." He turned toward Paige, who held out her hand. Max shook it, sealing the deal to have her represent Roth.

Paige stepped in front of Roth's chair, wedging her body like a shield between him and the detectives. "I'm advising my client to keep silent at this time. Until I've had a chance to talk to him at length."

"We'll be in touch," Sanchez said, handing Paige her

business card and peering around Paige at Roth. "If you've done nothing wrong, you have nothing to fear, Mr. Rothman."

Roth saw Max's fists clench. "My nephew did nothing but help."

Paige put her hand on Max's shoulder. "That's enough, Mr. Rothman. I'll take it from now on."

In his chair, Roth didn't relax. His "heroism" had turned into suspicious behavior in an instant. He knew the cops would start investigating him. And he knew that he wasn't, as Paige had assumed, a juvenile. He was eighteen. And even though he'd done nothing wrong this time, he might, because of circumstance, very well be in for a world of hurt.

"Here, drink this." Apocalypse handed Executioner a glass containing an inch of amber liquid. They were in Apocalypse's living room, alone in the empty house.

"What is it?"

"A shot of my father's finest Kentucky bourbon. To celebrate our victory."

Executioner took the glass, hands shaking so violently that the alcohol almost spilled.

"What's your problem?" Apocalypse's hands were rock steady. "You never drank booze before?"

"Beer," Executioner said. "Adrenaline rush. I'm trying to get over the rush." That part was a lie. Executioner felt like vomiting and was grateful that Apocalypse backed off from making any snide remarks.

"Drink it down. Has a calming effect."

Executioner did, despite fiery throat burn and watery eyes. The stuff tasted awful. "You drink this much?"

"Whenever I can sneak it. Dad rides herd on his liquor."

"You like it?"

"I love it."

Executioner had to admit that the hit of strong alcohol did calm nerves. The sharp edge of fear from what they'd done that morning was growing fuzzy. "We did pull it off, didn't we?"

"Like pros."

"Now what?"

"Now we wait and see how it washes out."

"But you're sure no one will know it was us . . . ?"

"Just so long as we keep our mouths shut. You get that part, don't you?"

Executioner saw a look of coldness in Apocalypse's blue eyes. "I get it."

Apocalypse raised a glass and clinked it against Executioner's. "Till death do us part."

17

Morgan awoke in the dark, her heart hammering and raw fear clogging her throat. Her eyes were tightly bandaged, and she couldn't open them. She cried out and a hand slid over hers. "It's all right, honey. I'm here," her mother's voice said. "Right here. You're in the hospital, and you're safe."

"What—" Morgan rasped.

"There was an explosion at your school. You have a concussion and bruises from flying hunks of concrete, but no broken bones. Do you remember anything?"

Morgan whimpered. Pictures flashed in her mind. Sitting on the wall. Laughing. Talking. A flash of white light. "Some." Her voice sounded hoarse to her own ears. "When?"

"It happened yesterday morning."

"Yesterday!"

"You're alive. Happy Thanksgiving." Her mother smoothed Morgan's cheek, kissed her forehead. "Thank God."

"My eyes . . ."

"Your eyes were damaged in the explosion. Chemical burns, a lot of debris from the concrete got into them. That's why they're covered. The ophthalmologist, Dr. Harvey, has applied antibiotic creams and thinks your vision will be fine, but for now, for a while, he wants to protect your eyes and keep them covered."

"How long?"

"A few weeks."

Morgan went cold all over. "Weeks?"

She felt her mother's fingers travel down her arm and grasp her hand. "You're going to be all right. That's what's important."

"What kind of explosion?"

"They're still investigating."

"I—I don't want to be blind."

"You won't be. This is just until you heal."

"I want to go home. When can I go home?"

"Maybe in a few days. Your scans and X-rays indicate no internal damage even though you were sitting so close to the blast. Your doctors just want to monitor you for a while longer. Keep track of your vitals. You have pain medication in your IV so you won't hurt. If you want more, if you want anything, just tell me."

Morgan's brain was spinning from the flood of information. "Trent . . . my friends. How are my friends? We were all together. Then there was a light . . . a noise . . . like a roar. . . ."

"Shhh," Paige said soothingly. "Don't think about that now. Just rest."

Morgan felt her mother tuck the bedcovers around her, cocooning her into the bed. "I don't want to be alone," Morgan cried.

"Not to worry. Your father or I will be with you every minute. Your hospital room has a sleeper chair that stretches out into a bed. One of us will be here as long as you're in the hospital. I promise. If you wake up scared, just call out and we'll be awake in seconds."

Morgan felt like a baby. Her senses were jumbled, everything unfamiliar except for her mother's soft perfume. "You won't leave me."

"Never. Now get some sleep."

Morgan was already feeling the effects of her exertion and the numbing medicine. She was suddenly exhausted. She sank into a pillow, her mother's hand wound tightly around hers. Paige's hand was an anchor, a lifeline to a world that Morgan could no longer see. She was adrift on a sea of closing darkness. As she drifted off it struck her that her mother hadn't answered her question about her friends. She tried to ask it again, but the words were tangled around her tongue and sleep was pulling her backward into its dark arms.

Morgan heard someone whispering her name softly into her ear. "Trent?" she said anxiously. "Is that you?"

"Shhh. Let's not wake your mother. She's asleep in a chair, real close to your bed."

Morgan's heart leaped. "Oh, Trent, thank God you're with me." She fumbled one hand in front of her.

"I'm right here," he said, catching her hand. His was as cool as the air.

Relief and gratitude welled up inside her. Tears dampened the bandages on her eyes. "Oh my God, I—I didn't know what happened to you. Are you here in the hospital?"

"Down the hall."

"Are you all right?"

"Some scrapes and bruises, but I'm good."

She opened her arms. "Hold me."

His arms wrapped around her and she leaned against his chest, but he still felt cool to her skin. "Are you cold?" she asked.

"This whole hospital is cold."

"I'm just so glad you're here with me. Do you know what happened?"

"Not really."

"We were at school. You were hugging me," she whispered. "I—I think I saw something under the staircase. Can't remember . . ." Feeling a headache building, she squeezed her eyes, which left them stinging and burning beneath the bandages.

"You hurting?" he asked, concern in his voice.

"A little. I keep trying to remember something."

"Don't force it." She felt him withdrawing. "I better

go," he said. "I don't want to get caught by the nurses either. Maybe we should keep this little visit our secret, so we don't get into trouble."

She saw the logic in his suggestion. "Will you come back?"

"Every chance I get."

"I love you, Trent."

"Love you too, babe."

The room fell silent and she knew he had gone. All she heard were sounds from machines and heat registers and her mother's light snoring. With her teeth chattering, Morgan snuggled back down under the covers. She felt helpless. She was cold and blind, but knowing that Trent was in the immediate vicinity comforted her. And if he was able to sneak past her sleeping mother, he was pretty stealthy, so she was sure he'd do it again. She sighed and fell asleep secure in that thought.

She awoke to the feel of a blood pressure cuff being tightened on her upper arm. "Just taking your vitals," a voice said. "I'm Mary Lou, your day nurse."

"Is it daytime?" Morgan's world was dark.

"Friday morning," the nurse said.

"My mother—"

"Ran down to the cafeteria. Said she'd be right back."

"Is the sun shining?"

"Off and on. Do you need some help with your breakfast? You have a trayful of food."

The smell of food drifted to Morgan. She was hungry,

but had no idea of how to handle a tray she couldn't see. Was someone going to have to feed her as if she were a baby? "I'll wait for Mom."

The nurse slid a banana into Morgan's hand. "Good source of potassium. You should be able to handle this on your own."

The shape of the fruit was familiar, but without seeing it, Morgan had no idea how ripe it might be. She only liked bananas when they were just turning yellow, barely sweet. Without her eyesight, she felt useless. "Maybe later."

"An occupational therapist will be in later this morning," the nurse said brightly.

"A what?"

"A therapist. A person who'll help you cope while the bandages are in place on your eyes. Just some pointers and coping skills. It'll be very helpful."

"But the bandages are temporary."

"True, but you still want to be able to feed yourself and handle personal hygiene, don't you?"

Morgan couldn't dispute that. She didn't like being helpless and dependent, no matter how short the time it would take for her corneas to heal. "All right," she said, feeling tears rising behind her bandages. "I guess it will help me."

"Of course it will."

Morgan raised the banana to her nose, sniffed and discovered the scent strong, full. The skin felt thick and she guessed it was less to the ripe side than the overripe side. Bravely she found the correct end and broke the skin. She slowly lowered the peel from all sides and ate the perfectly delicious piece of fruit.

She was munching dry cereal when her mother breezed into the room. "I'm sorry it's taken me so long. The cafeteria line was a mile long."

"It's okay. I'm just groping my way through breakfast."

"You made a joke. You must be feeling better."

Morgan wanted to say that her nocturnal visit from Trent had made the difference in her outlook, but she kept her promise to him and said nothing.

"You want milk on that cereal?" Paige asked.

"I wasn't sure I could pour it without spilling. Chewing it dry is fine. I'll drink the milk afterward. It all goes to the same place, doesn't it?"

Paige laughed and Morgan liked the sound of it. "Where's Dad?"

"He's in the office dealing with piled-up work. He'll sleep here tonight and I'll work tomorrow."

"I guess this is a big mess for you attorneys."

"Everyone's scrambling. The only thing the cops are certain of is that a bomb went off. No leads yet on who might have done it."

Someone set a bomb? At Edison? On *purpose*? "Why? Who would do that?"

"That's a mystery."

"Tell me what you know," Morgan said. "Kids must have been hurt."

"Thirty-seven were wounded, not all seriously, though."

Paige was going to back into the statistics, Morgan realized. "And what else?"

"Seven people are still in the hospital."

"And?" She urged her mother to tell her everything and steeled herself for what might be coming.

"And nine people died—seven students, two teachers." Paige's voice caught. "You were so lucky."

Morgan felt nauseous. "Who?"

"A history teacher. Principal Simmons. He was just coming down the stairs when the explosion happened. The staircase fell."

Morgan began to tremble. Simmons was a good guy. She saw him in her mind's eye pushing his glasses up on his nose, as was his habit. "And the kids?"

"Perhaps now isn't the time—"

"Tell me!" She flung the miniature cereal box across the room. "My friends? Oh my God! Where's Kelli?" Morgan recalled that Kelli had been sitting, sullen and uncommunicative, farther down the wall from her and Trent.

Paige grabbed Morgan's hands. "No, no. It's all right. Kelli was hurt—a concussion, several broken ribs—but she's going to be fine."

Weak with relief, Morgan sagged. "Where is she?"

"Upstairs on another floor."

"I want to see her. I want to visit her. Take me to her."

"And you will. She's fine, honey. Really." Paige paused, squeezed Morgan's hands. "Unfortunately, though, she lost her baby."

18

"So how's the local hero?"

Roth glanced up at Liza as she marched into his living room. He was stretched out on the sofa, bundled in Carla's quilts, holding a joystick and firing torpedoes at alien life-forms on the TV screen. He pressed the pause button to hold his place in the game. "He's crazy bored."

"How are your hands? Look hammered-up to me."

Band-Aids covered the worst of the deep cuts. He'd torn a fingernail off digging through the rubble and needed ten stitches in one palm. His forehead had taken five stitches to repair. "The scars will give me character."

The coffee table was laid out with snacks, drinks, books and a pile of game cards. "How can you be bored? Looks like you've got everything you need right here."

"Everything except my freedom. Max took my keys,

won't let me drive for another few days." He held up a fruit platter. "Want some health food?"

Relieved that Roth was talking to her after the argument they'd had in her bedroom weeks before, Liza sat in the recliner beside the sofa. She'd had to suck up her courage to drop by unannounced, afraid he might have told her not to come over if she'd called first. She'd been frantic to see him, to know he was all right.

"I want to apologize for what I said—" she started.

He waved her off. "I shouldn't have gotten so twisted up about it. After this bombing, it doesn't seem important, does it?"

She agreed with a rush of gratitude. She hated being estranged from Roth. "Max and Carla at the shop?" she asked, changing the subject.

"Yes." They had gone to work at the Ink Spot for the first time in four days. The whole town was in mourning, but things were beginning to settle down. Life went on, no matter how heavy the losses. "What've you been doing now that school's shut down?" Edison was closed until further notice. Makeup days would be tacked onto the end of the school term.

"I've been to two funerals and a memorial service."

"Sorry," Roth said. "Were they friends?"

"No. I didn't know the kids who were buried, but I felt like I should go. Popular kids have lots of kids who attend their funerals, but the not-so-popular ones? Not so much. Crappy way to go out. One girl was buried on her thirteenth birthday."

Roth spat out a swearword, turned on his game and killed several more aliens before pausing again.

"Feel better?" she asked.

"No."

"You hear anything . . . you know, about suspects?"

He put the joystick on the coffee table. He wasn't ready to say he might be a suspect. "Just what's on the news. Sick of the talking heads hashing it over. How about you?"

"Drove past the school yesterday. The cops and crime scene people are still crawling all over the place. FBI too. Bombs are taken real seriously."

Roth recalled his fireworks prank. Stupid of him. Nothing funny about things blowing up. "Were you there the day it happened?"

"I was standing across the street finishing up a cig. I had a note from home, though, so I wasn't in any hurry to get to class. I saw you running toward the front door." She almost added, *I didn't want you to go inside,* but didn't.

"I was running at first because I was late, and I *didn't* have a note," he said. "So you saw the atrium explode from across the street?"

"Boom," she said. "Scared the crap out of me."

"What did you do?"

"Just stood and watched the building clear. I wanted to run too, but it was like I was glued in place. Couldn't move my feet. Kids were running and screaming, but I was in a trance. Nothing seemed real even though I saw all this dust and glass shoot from the atrium. The kids, the ones who got out, well, we all just stood there staring like it wasn't really happening. The cops had the place surrounded in no time and finally they herded us all onto buses and drove us to the civic auditorium. Our parents came to pick us up if we weren't hurt. You were busy rescuing people, so you missed the roundup."

"It was one hell of a day." Roth ran his hands through his hair. "You been by the hospital?"

Liza's radar went up. "I haven't seen your girlfriend, if that's what you're asking."

"Knock it off. Morgan's not my girlfriend. I'm just trying to keep track of the kids I helped."

Liza bit her tongue. She didn't want out of his good graces again. "Okay, sorry. Cheap shot. Just not used to thinking of you as a Rescue Ranger." She took a deep breath, decided to make a peace offering. "Would you like me to drive you over to the hospital so you can check in on her yourself?" *Please say no. . . .*

She saw anticipation spring into Roth's eyes. "You'd do that?"

Disappointed by his reaction, she shrugged with pretended indifference. "Got nothing else to do."

"Let me do a couple of things first. Back in a jiff." He threw back the quilts.

She'd been the one to make the offer, so she had no one to blame except herself for his taking her up on it. "You going to call Max and Carla to let them know we're leaving the house?"

"Easier to get forgiveness than permission," Roth said, pushing himself off the sofa.

Liza watched him limp from the room, wondering with all her heart if he'd have gone to see her if she'd been the one hospitalized.

"You want to come up?" Roth asked once he and Liza were in the hospital lobby.

"Don't want to crash your reunion."

"Your call."

"Some other time," she said, backing away. She grabbed a seat and started thumbing through a three-year-old magazine from a nearby table as if it were just off the rack.

"I won't take long."

"I'll wait here." She blinked back stinging tears but never looked up.

Roth ducked into the hospital's gift shop and looked around for some small gift so that he wouldn't show up in Morgan's room empty-handed. The store was full of chintzy junk that made him gag, but he finally settled on a small stuffed dog. It was meant for young children, but so what? He knew girls liked stuffed animals. He paid for it, crossed to the information desk and asked for Morgan's room number. During his elevator ride to the fifth floor, he wasn't remembering Morgan covered with cement dust and debris from the explosion. He was remembering her at the homecoming dance, twirling on the stadium grass in the moonlight. He was seeing her face turned up to his, her lips moist and soft, her hair spilling around her shoulders and his fingers tugging through the long strands.

When he arrived at her room, he paused, peered in. Morgan was sitting upright in the bed, a tray table in front

of her with an assortment of objects on it. She was finger-
ing each object, carefully defining it in her hands, then
putting it down and moving on to the next item. It was
then that he saw that her eyes were bandaged. Shock hit
him like a wall. For a moment, he teetered, undecided
about entering the room. Without warning, her head
lifted and her face turned toward the door. "Who's there?
I know someone's there. Who is it?"

Making up his mind in an instant, he went inside. "It's
Stuart Rothman."

"Roth?"

"One and the same."

Morgan held out her hands. This was the person who'd
made her emotions go haywire for months, and now here
he was. She had no way of knowing what she looked like at
the moment, but she was sure that she in no way resem-
bled the girl he'd been with on the night of the dance. "Oh,
Roth . . . I—I didn't know . . . I can't see. . . ."

"Your eyes—"

"Temporary," she said quickly. "That's what my doctor
believes. I was looking right at the bomb when it went off.
I didn't even have time to blink."

"But you're going to be all right?"

"That's what I'm being told. What about you?"

"Stitches. A few cuts and bruises. Banged up a leg
crawling over chunks of concrete. I'm fine."

She asked, "Do you mind if I hold your hand? It helps
ground me, so I'm not floating in a void with voices coming out of nowhere."

Of course he didn't mind. "Suits me."

She took hold of his hand, which was covered with a large gauze bandage. "Mom told me that you were the one who pulled me out. She said that the rest of the staircase fell just after you did. Thank you for saving me."

Self-conscious, he shrugged, then realized she couldn't see any of his gestures or movements. "I saw your red hair under a pile of junk. If you hadn't had that red hair, I would have missed you." He playfully tugged on a generous hank of her hair. "I'm glad you're all right." After a moment of embarrassed silence, he asked, "So what's with all this stuff on the tray?"

"Therapy," she said, glad for the distraction. She ran her free hand over a couple of objects. "Hairbrush, toothbrush, makeup brush. I need to figure out how to do things for myself until the bandages come off."

"Makes sense."

"Why would someone do this, Roth? Why would anyone blow up our school? What did we do to deserve such hate?" Her voice caught, trembled, the magnitude of the disaster descending on her like an anvil.

"I guess that's the million-dollar question."

"People died, Roth. They died!"

He slipped his arm around her, rested his cheek on the crown of her head. He felt her stiffen, then relax and lean into him. "The cops and the FBI will figure it out. They'll catch the jerks who did this." He didn't add that he was somehow a suspect. And Paige, as his attorney, obviously hadn't mentioned it either.

She felt warm and safe in his arms. Guiltily she remembered that Trent was just down the hall and pulled away. "Tissue, please."

He passed her the box from the bedside table. She fumbled, pulled out several, held the wad against her bandaged eyes. "I keep crying and soaking my bandages." She laughed self-consciously. "I'm driving the nurses crazy, making them change my bandages all the time." She eased back onto the pillows.

He wanted to soothe her, make her feel better. He remembered the toy dog he'd bought, fished it out of the pocket of his hoodie. "I brought you something to keep you company." He set the dog in her hand.

She turned it over, sniffed the freshness and newness of the fuzzy material, rubbed it against her cheek. "A dog?"

"Bingo."

She laughed. "That'll be his name—B-I-N-G-O. Thank you." She hugged the stuffed animal to her. "What color is he?"

"White. Black ears and nose. Red tongue."

"I love him."

Roth's eyes swept over her. No need to pretend now. He could look at her all he wanted because she wouldn't know. "Can I come visit you again?"

"I'm supposed to be going home tomorrow. But you can come to my house and visit me anytime."

"I might do that." He silently swore that he would.

She rested the stuffed dog on her chest and continued to stroke its softness. "One thing I'm grateful for, though."

"What's that?"

"At least my friends made it through. I'm so happy they're all safe."

Roth straightened, reeled slightly as realization washed over him. He clenched his jaw. She didn't know! No one had told her. Morgan didn't know!

19

"I'm sorry, Morgan. Really sorry I didn't tell you before now. Will you forgive me?"

The plea came from Kelli. Her mother had brought her down from her room to Morgan's room in a wheelchair because that was hospital protocol. Jane and Paige had left the room, leaving the girls alone. Seeing her friend in the bed, eyes bandaged, broke Kelli's heart, made her feel guiltier than she already did. "How are you?" Kelli asked.

"I'll be all right. What about you?"

"They said I'll be fine. I ache all over, but I'm going home today."

"Wish I were," Morgan said. "Why didn't you tell me? We've been friends forever, and yet you couldn't confide in me that you were pregnant?"

"I—I don't know. I was so ashamed, I guess. I mean, Mark dumped me like a bad dream when I told him in

August. I kept telling myself that I could change his mind. That I could make him want to get married. I couldn't."

"Did Trent know?" If he did, Morgan was going to skewer him the next time he visited her in the night.

"I don't know. Guys don't talk to other guys like girls—" She stopped. "I mean, like girls are *supposed* to talk."

"And all the times I asked you, 'What's wrong?', you just pushed me away."

"I wanted to tell you more than anything. I started to a hundred times. When Mom found out, she made me swear to keep it a secret. But I should never have kept it from you."

Morgan picked at the bedcovers, needing something to do with her hands. She longed to see people's expressions when they spoke. Without her sight it was like filling in a puzzle piece that didn't exist. She could fall back on images of people she knew, but with strangers, she had no road map, no way to gather an image except through their voices and touch. In many ways Kelli was a stranger to her at the moment. "How did she find out?"

"You know Mom." Kelli offered a short derisive laugh. "She watches my weight like a hawk. She saw I was gaining around the middle."

Morgan had seen it too but had said nothing. She should have. She'd watched Kelli change right before her eyes but had been too caught up in her own life to press her friend very hard. She realized she shared some of the blame for Kelli's silence. "I might have helped you figure it out," she mumbled. "I should have helped you."

"Once Mom figured it out, I was almost five months along. I'd already made up my mind I was going to have the baby. What I hadn't decided was what I was going to do after he was born."

"You were going to have a boy?"

"Yes." Kelli's voice quavered. "But I didn't know it was a boy until . . ." Her voice trailed off, ebbed into a heavy silence. Morgan felt Kelli's pain and loss. "Mom took me to a free clinic in Grand Rapids because I hadn't been going to a doctor."

"Not at all?"

"Denial isn't just a river in Egypt." Kelli quoted the old joke. She forced herself to smile, but realized Morgan couldn't see her effort.

"And after he was born, what were you going to do?"

Kelli didn't answer right away, and when she did, Morgan heard the resignation in her tone. "There were only two choices—keep him and raise him or put him up for adoption. I kept bouncing between the two. Couldn't decide. One day I wanted to raise him. The next day I wanted to give him up."

"What did Mark want?"

Kelli took a deep rattling breath. "He said he didn't care, but I knew he wanted me to give him up. Mark said that he loved me, but that nothing was going to derail his plans for a football career."

Morgan heard the forlorn hopelessness in Kelli's voice. The words made her mad. How could Mark be so cruel? "And your mother?"

"Adoption." Kelli's voice fell to a whisper. "No one wanted him except me."

"I'm really sorry, Kelli." Morgan held out her hands and was rewarded by Kelli grasping them tightly.

"Doesn't make any difference now, does it? I lost the baby. And Mark's going to be a paraplegic for the rest of his life."

Morgan already knew Mark's fate—her mother had told her yesterday—but sorrow in Kelli's voice made fresh tears well up and spill into the bandages on her eyes.

"Why did this happen, Morgan? Why did someone set off a bomb and change all our lives?"

Morgan had no answers. She tugged Kelli out of the wheelchair and pulled her onto the bed with her. The friends wrapped their arms around each other and cried for what was gone and for what could never be again.

Morgan went home on Monday, five days after the bombing. She was both happy and scared about going home, away from the security of the nurses. Her dad took her on a tour of the house, with her holding his elbow as the therapist had trained her to do when she was being led. The trainer had given her one of the sticks used by blind people. She used it gingerly, halfheartedly, self-conscious about the red-tipped stick that announced she couldn't see. Inside the house, her father insisted that she use it.

"This is just temporary," he kept saying. "The bandages won't be on forever."

Weeks seemed like an eternity to Morgan at the moment.

"I picked up in every room," Paige said, following along behind, then walking beside and finally in front of Morgan and Hal as they toured. "Nothing to trip you up, honey."

Morgan made a complete circuit of the first floor and stopped at the stairs. "I don't need help to get up to my room," she said, grabbing hold of the banister and dropping her dad's arm.

"Maybe you shouldn't—"

"Mom . . . I can do this." The therapist had been very clear with Morgan's parents about allowing her to navigate her own path through the days of darkness and letting her choose what she felt comfortable doing. It wasn't as if she'd been blind since birth. She had been part of the seeing world and would be again. All she needed were basics to help her through the short haul. "You and Dad have to go back to work."

"Not right away."

"We can hire a helper," Hal said. "You don't need to be alone."

Morgan knew her parents were anxious to fence her in, keep her safe. She didn't want to be afraid either, but when she'd been a kid learning how to ride a bike, she got back on it immediately no matter how many times she fell, no matter how many scrapes she received. "I know how to make a sandwich, get around the house, go to the bathroom by myself, wipe my backside—"

"No need to enumerate your skills," Paige said, cutting Morgan off. "We get the message."

Hal chuckled.

Morgan stepped onto the stairs she'd once crawled up as an infant, grasped the rail with both hands. By the time she reached the top, she'd figured out her pace, the width and height of each step. At the top she felt her way along the wall to her bedroom, opened the door and was rewarded by a familiar sense of comfort and belonging. Her parents followed behind her.

"Uh-oh," Paige muttered.

Hal cleared his throat awkwardly.

"What's happening?" Morgan asked.

"Um . . . I put up a banner and helium balloons to welcome you home, but . . . ," Paige said meekly.

"But I can't see them."

"A miscalculation," Paige said contritely.

Morgan burst out laughing. She turned and opened her arms and the three of them stood hugging and laughing until they were weeping with the absurdity of a mother's carefully planned homecoming for the daughter who could not see it.

20

Morgan woke that night to the sound of Trent whispering her name. She bolted upright in bed. "Trent?"

"None other."

Incredulous, she asked, "How did you get in?"

"Climbed," he said.

"To the second floor?" He'd never done that in the past. He'd always just tossed grit at her window until she opened it, then she'd meet him under their tree.

"Well, I can't fly," he said.

"But—but Dad put up storm windows. And Mom always locks them."

"Must have forgotten this one. Hey, aren't you glad I'm here?"

"Oh yes." She opened her arms, still warm from being under her covers. She held him. "You're cold as ice."

"Yeah. Cold climb. Maybe I could get under the covers with you."

Tempting. "Can I trust you?"

"Babe! You wound me. Of course you can trust me."

She scooted over, but snuggling up to him proved difficult because it felt so strange to have him in her bed. "How are you doing?"

"Hanging in."

"Sad about Mark, huh?"

Trent said nothing.

"Did you know Kelli was pregnant?"

Silence.

"Trent, talk to me. Tell me what you know."

"He didn't love her like I love you."

He always knew the right thing to say and what she needed to hear. "When this is over, when my bandages come off and we go back to school, how will Mark and Kelli . . . I mean, how will they . . . ?"

"Let's not talk about them," Trent said, his voice soft in her ear.

She didn't really want to talk about them either. She wanted the warmth and comfort of Trent's arms around her. She was afraid to ask him for too much physical contact because one thing could so easily lead to another, so she said, "If I fall asleep, please don't let my parents catch you in my room with me."

"It's a promise."

Her brain was growing fuzzy and sleep was coming for her. She hugged something close to her chest and with a start realized it was Bingo, the stuffed dog Roth had given her. His image unfolded in her mind's eye. Roth, darkly dressed, full lips and amazing blue eyes, looking as if he wanted to kiss her. Guilt shot through her like a cannonball. What was wrong with her? How could she be lying under the covers with one boy while her memory was clinging to another?

"I'm bored." Apocalypse stopped shooting fire bursts at the demons on the TV screen and tossed aside the game controller.

"Why? Because I'm winning?" Executioner asked.

"I've won ten rounds to your three," Apocalypse said. "This is such baby stuff after setting off a real bomb."

They were alone in the house, parents at work, nothing to do without school to attend. Outside, an early December storm had turned the world and landscape white with snow.

Executioner was bored too, having been visiting and gaming since early that morning. But also scared. It had been ten days since the bomb, and cops and FBI were sniffing around and checking out people all over town. The explosion was all anyone talked about. It had made national news shows, but the cameras and crews were gone now, so only the local stations were left to keep the story alive.

"They're going to interview everybody who goes to Edison, you know," Executioner said.

"So?"

"What if they want to interview us?"

Apocalypse gave Executioner a cold hard stare. "Don't be such a *girl*. If you get hauled in, you lie. Got that? You do know how to lie, don't you?"

Executioner colored under the other's withering stare. "I'm just saying that maybe we should be doing something to make them ignore us and home in on somebody else. That way they'd never get to us."

Apocalypse started to say something, stopped, gave Executioner a thoughtful look. "An intervention. That's not a half-bad idea."

Executioner almost fell over from the faint bit of praise. "I was thinking it over last night. Thought of a few names. Kids who get into trouble regularly."

Apocalypse studied the ceiling. "It wouldn't take much to turn the cops on to someone. They really want to solve this and haul someone's ass away."

"Yeah. That's just what I was thinking too."

Apocalypse flashed an expression that said, *I doubt it*, but Executioner saw the wheels of mischief were turning in the other's head. "We need a list."

Executioner leaned back feeling pleased. Very pleased indeed.

Max put Roth to work in his shop just as soon as Roth grew too restless to stay put at home. He was bored and wanted to see Morgan again. She had invited him to come by her house, but he had stayed away, unsure if she had really meant the invitation and because he didn't want to ruffle

Paige's feathers. She might not like Morgan associating with someone she was defending.

Paige had called once and asked to drop by to talk and update Max, Carla and Roth on the investigation. She arrived one evening in a cloud of snow, wrapped in fur.

"I like your coat," Carla said, taking it from her and shaking off the wet snow.

"I know wearing fur offends some people, but it's warm," Paige said.

"Doesn't offend me," Carla said. "Coffee?"

"Sure."

Max took her into the living room and offered her his favorite recliner. She chose the dining table, with the three of them sitting across from her. Roth got the message that this wasn't a social call.

"How's Morgan?" Roth asked at the first opportunity.

"She's doing well. Thanks for asking."

Roth wanted Morgan to be safe, and he didn't want Paige to know his concern transcended casual interest.

"The police will call to question you," Paige said, opening her briefcase and removing a file folder. "FBI, maybe."

Roth read his name across the tab, swallowed hard, felt his palms grow damp.

"They'll want you to come down to the station—their turf, their rules. Don't go without contacting me. Don't act belligerent; be cooperative, and don't say anything unless I'm with you."

"Why am I in trouble?" Roth wanted to know.

She flipped open the folder. "You have a little history of run-ins with the police."

"Kid stuff," Max said defensively. "He was never charged. I'd just go to the station and pick him up when the cops called. Nobody branded him as a bad kid, just a troubled one."

"History is history."

Roth slouched, grew pensive thinking about all the early trouble he caused for Max—petty stuff like fights, truancy, writing graffiti on walls. "I've been walking the line for four years. Doesn't that count for anything?"

Paige glanced up at him. "Cops see what they want to see. Catching the bomber is a top priority. They're going to look hard at you."

Carla reached over and patted Roth's hands, which were folded on the table. He wanted to pound the surface with his fists. "He's going to graduate this year. And his grades are Bs and Cs." She said it proudly and Roth wished she hadn't. Paige had a daughter who never saw a C on her report statement and probably very few Bs.

Paige looked unimpressed and unfazed. "Plus you're eighteen. An adult in the eyes of the law."

"Can't help that," Roth said.

"And you ran into the school building."

"Well, doesn't *that* seem suspicious," Max barked.

"He's a hero," Carla protested.

"I think he is too. He saved my daughter. She would have died if he hadn't acted the way he did," Paige said, "but everything is under scrutiny."

132

Roth felt color creep up his neck. "They're prejudiced. I don't look like an all-American boy to them, do I?" He pushed up his long-sleeved shirt, exposing the tats on his wrist and forearm, a colorful, fiery dragon that twisted its ascent all the way to his shoulder.

"I own an ink shop," Max interjected. "I do body art. It's logical he'd have some tats."

Paige closed the folder, looked straight into Roth's eyes. "I'm your attorney, Roth. I believe you. But I must also defend you. Is there anything you're holding back? Anything I need to know?"

His heart skipped a few beats and his insides turned watery. "Like what?"

"You tell me. Once we get into that interrogation room, I don't want any surprises coming from the police."

There was his fireworks prank. Few people knew about it, though—Liza, because he'd told her, and Morgan, because she'd figured it out. His heart sank. No telling if Morgan might spill the beans to her mother. For a moment he almost confessed, but something turned inside of him. The information would only make him look more guilty. He met her gaze. "Nothing I can think of right now." A lie, but for the time being, it was his secret to keep.

21

Roth took to driving by Morgan's house, the desire to see her growing more intense as the days pushed closer to Christmas. Her house sat far back on a sloping lawn studded with trees in a wealthier Grandville neighborhood. Just days before Christmas, with snow a foot deep and the sun sparkling off the pristine whiteness, he slowed his truck to a crawl as he passed the large piece of property. And that was when he saw her. She stood under a massive tree gesturing with her hands into what seemed like empty air. He braked and stared.

The tree was leafless, its bare branches stretching high into bright blue sky. He saw Morgan quite clearly. She looked to be talking and gesturing into thin air. Chills went up his spine. What the heck was she doing? He watched for a few minutes, but when she turned toward the house, he put his truck into gear and turned into the long driveway. His tires crunched over the salt and sand used to clear the most recent snowfall.

Morgan held the red-tipped stick in front of her, moving it expertly from side to side. She made the front porch before she heard his tires. "Who's there?" she called out.

Roth shut off the engine and climbed out of his truck. "Roth," he answered. "I was out doing stuff and thought I'd come by and say hi."

She wore sunglasses over her bandaged eyes, and it was obvious that he'd caught her off guard. "Oh. Hello."

He bounded onto the porch and fought an urge to pity her in her blindness. Her cheeks were red with the cold and she looked vulnerable, not at all like the self-confident girl he'd known at school. "It's cold out here. Maybe we should go inside."

"Well, I . . . I mean, nobody's home except me." A dumb thing to announce, she thought, but his unplanned arrival had thrown her off balance.

"Then I'll leave."

She caught his arm. "No. Don't go. Come in and I'll fix us some hot chocolate."

"Sounds good to me."

She surprised herself with the invitation, but in all honesty she craved the company.

He followed her inside her house, down a hallway of dark wood floors, past rooms of understated fine furniture and into an industrial-style kitchen with gleaming appliances. He thought how much Carla would like a house like this.

"Sit," Morgan said, motioning toward a table. She knew every inch of the house after spending two weeks alone inside and getting acquainted with it via her other senses. Sounds bounced around her with a quality that offered direction; smells were intensified, leading her like invisible fingers; touch helped her to appreciate the house's walls, curves, textures.

Roth sat, fighting the urge to offer help. He figured she wouldn't have asked to make hot chocolate if she couldn't do it. "How are you doing?" he asked while she worked.

"I'm getting the bandages off next week, two days before Christmas. Can't wait."

"All right," he said with a grin she couldn't see.

"How about you? Your hands healed?"

"They're fine. A few wicked scars, though. Makes me look tough."

She mused, "I've always thought you looked tough."

"Yeah, big bad Roth." He watched her move around the kitchen with confidence. Everything in the cupboards and silverware drawers and on the pots-and-pans shelves had a proper place and her hands were sure and quick. She fumbled very little and in minutes had measured out two cups of milk with a special measuring device into a pot on the stove. She sprinkled in powdered chocolate with a set of measuring spoons and stirred the concoction, held a hand over the pot every so often until she was satisfied with the temperature, then poured the mixture into two ceramic cups. She didn't spill a drop. "I'm impressed," he said as she carried the cups to the table. He took one; she set the other down and pulled out a chair for herself.

Her accomplishment impressed her too. She'd never performed a ritual for anyone except her parents, and having Roth materialize so suddenly had unnerved her. How much had he seen and overheard? "Hours of practice," she said. "Not much else to do until the bandages come off. I still have Christmas shopping to do. Kelli and I are going to the mall after my eye doctor appointment. Girls' day out." Her friend wasn't over losing the baby or Mark's terrible injury.

Roth had always taken his sight for granted. Most people did. "What are you looking forward to most?"

"Reading. Plus I'm getting a car for Christmas." She smiled, absolute glee on her face.

"Awesome."

"I know it's because Mom and Dad feel so sorry for me. I haven't whined, haven't complained," she added, "but I don't want to discourage them either. I'd love my own car!"

"Wheels mean freedom," Roth said in agreement.

Trent would love for Morgan to have a car of her own too. He'd told her so just that morning. Just as soon as that thought came to her, Morgan was swamped with guilt. If she cared so much about Trent, then why was she enjoying Roth's visit so much?

Roth watched the change in her demeanor from across the table. Was it something he'd said?

She put her hands around her cup, brought it up to her mouth and took a sip.

Roth saw the pearl ring Trent had given her on her finger. He didn't know how to ask her about Trent. He thought back to the scene he'd watched as she had stood under the tree. She'd appeared like an actress speaking lines, rehearsing a play for an invisible audience. It troubled him. "Hey, it's getting late. My uncle will be wondering where I am. I'm helping in his shop while we're out of school." He stood and she scrambled up too.

She wanted him to stay, but what if Trent came by again and found him there? "I'm glad you stopped by."

"Thanks for the chocolate." He started to the door and she followed after him. "I know the way," he said, wanting to save her the trip.

"Me too." In truth, she wanted his company as long as possible.

At the door, he stopped, lifted her chin, wishing he could search her eyes for some clue about what she was thinking and feeling.

Her heart raced and she wished she could see his face.

"I'll be glad when your bandages are off too," he said. "You have pretty eyes."

She felt a melting sensation but took a step backward. Trent loved her; Roth intrigued her. She felt a kinship with both of them. "Bye," she said.

He shut the door behind him, and she rested her forehead on the doorframe. Emotions she couldn't define careened through her. Seconds later she heard his truck pull away.

Roth turned out of the driveway, pulled over to the shoulder of the road and dug out his cell. Before he lost his courage, he called the Friersons' law firm. The secretary put him through to Paige as soon as he said his name.

Coming on the line, Paige asked, "Roth, what's up? Have the police called for an interview?"

"No, Counselor. I—um—I'm calling to let you know I stopped by your house and saw Morgan." *Easier to get forgiveness than permission,* he silently reminded himself.

"Okay," she said, drawing out the word. "Is anything wrong with Morgan?" Concern rose in her voice.

"She made us both hot chocolate. She did a really good job too."

"Why are you calling?"

He screwed up his courage and told her about what he'd witnessed beneath the tree on the front lawn. It was none of his business, but somehow it *was* his business. He was linked to Morgan.

Paige was silent, with only her breathing to let him know she was still on the line. Then realization hit Roth like a thrown brick. "She still doesn't know, does she?" He stopped. "How have you kept it from her?"

"With difficulty," Paige said softly.

"Crap!" He slammed his fist against his steering wheel, hesitating to say anything worse.

"You—you didn't say anything, did you?" Alarm pitched Paige's voice higher.

"No."

"Good call."

Roth didn't know if she was talking about revealing the front-lawn scene or keeping his mouth shut. "She should know," he said, tamping down his rising temper.

"My daughter. My timing. Goodbye, Roth."

After Paige hung up, Roth's temper boiled over. He shoved the truck into drive, peeled off the shoulder of the road and cursed a blue streak all the way back to his uncle's shop.

Morgan had her iPod earbuds planted firmly in her ears, listening to songs Trent had downloaded for her, when she felt a hand on her shoulder. She jumped and yanked out the tiny buds.

"Sorry," her mom said. "Didn't mean to startle you. I knocked, but you didn't answer."

Morgan calmed her racing heart, turned off the music. "No problem."

"Dad's with me too."

"Wow, you must have something big to say."

She felt their weight settle on her bed on either side of her. "Yes, we do."

"I'm not getting a car." Morgan expressed the biggest disappointment she could think of.

"We'll get you a car," Hal said to her left.

"Okay . . . then what's so serious?"

Paige closed her hand over Morgan's. "There's something we must tell you. Something hard. Something that's going to hurt."

Morgan's heart went into trip-hammer mode and a

hard knot formed in her stomach. What could be so bad? "Out with it. You're scaring me."

"It's . . . it's about Trent," Paige said.

Morgan groaned. They'd discovered he'd been sneaking into her room. "It isn't Trent's fault," Morgan said defensively. "I let him visit me."

Her mother's grip tightened on her hand. "Morgan, honey, please listen to me. There is no Trent. He . . . he died in the explosion."

22

"That's crazy talk," Morgan said, dismissing her mother on the spot. "He visits me all the time."

"No," Paige said. "He doesn't."

Morgan jerked her hand away from her mother's. "Why are you lying to me? I'm telling you, he's been here to see me."

Hal gently pulled her hands to his chest. "We should have told you sooner. I'm sorry we didn't tell you sooner."

Paige jumped in, saying, "You were so wounded, Morgan, both in body and spirit. I couldn't bear to tell you the truth. That's why we've waited."

"But I talk to him every day!" She grew braver. "Every night, he visits me. He visited me in the hospital."

"No. The doctor and nurses reported seeing you sitting up in bed, opening your arms and reaching out like you were trying to . . . to hold someone. We watched you with our own eyes. But no one was there. No one *is* there. Trent . . . died."

Morgan couldn't absorb what she was being told. Trent had talked to her. He'd held her, kissed her . . . hadn't he? "So I'm the crazy one?"

"No. You're projecting. You made him up because you needed to. One of your doctors, a psychiatrist, told us that your brain, your memories, were as bruised as your body. He suggested we give you space to work out the loss on your own. So we did. You were so fragile."

He couldn't be—mustn't be—gone. He couldn't be dead! "But I'm home! Why didn't you tell me this the minute I came home?"

"Cowardice. You were coping so well, progressing. I couldn't stand to see you crash."

Morgan pulled her arms free from her father, pummeled him, flailing and crying the whole time. Once her strength was spent, he pulled her close and soothed her.

"We were trying to protect you."

"Did Kelli know? Did the whole world know except me?" Her anger was replaced by despair. "Is that why Trent's parents never came to visit me?" She hadn't realized the last thing had been gnawing at her until the words spilled out of her mouth. She liked them; they liked her. Why hadn't they come?

"They *did* come, but you were out of it. And they were dealing with their own grief, the wrongness of his dying. They've called to check on you a few times."

Morgan couldn't believe everyone had so carefully and

ruthlessly kept Trent's death a secret from her. It wasn't fair! "You should have told me! How did you hide it for so long?"

"We begged everyone who came to visit you to say nothing. We kept the TV turned off in your room while you were in and out of consciousness. The media stopped listing the names of the deceased after two days, so we felt as if you wouldn't hear the names even when you began recovering. And because of your eyes, you couldn't read a paper or surf the Web."

"But I didn't know the truth!" Fresh tears flowed with her recriminations.

"You never once asked us about him. You never said, 'I talked to Trent today.'" Paige's voice went soft and sad.

That stopped Morgan cold. She hadn't asked—not point-blank, anyway. *How are my friends?* was what she'd asked. And according to Paige and Hal, the visits, the manifestations of Trent's presence, were all illusions, self-created and self-fulfilled. Resignation and defensiveness hit her at the same time. "I didn't ask because he was coming to visit me."

"Oh, honey . . . ," Paige said, smoothing Morgan's hair. "I'm so sorry."

Morgan pulled free of Hal's embrace. Why should she be alive and Trent be gone forever? She'd been sitting next to him on the wall. How could she have lived and he have died? It wasn't right. Her eyes stung from the salt of her tears, and her face felt puffy and wet.

Paige said, "Let me rebandage your eyes."

Morgan was too drained to move.

"You'll regain your sight. Things will be better," Hal offered.

"We love you, Morgan," Paige said.

She sat numbly on the bed with her dad holding her hand while her mother left to gather gauze and tape. Hal talked soothingly, but his words didn't register with her. She felt sick to her stomach, and cold, so very cold. Morgan struggled to button down her pain. How could she have allowed her mind to trick her? How could she have pretended Trent into existence with such veracity that she'd had whole conversations with a dead person? Wasn't this the definition of insanity?

When Paige returned and began to apply fresh bandages, Morgan asked, "Did Trent's parents bury him?"

Paige's moving fingers paused, then quickly resumed their work. "Yes, but we're going to have a memorial service as soon as you feel up to it. When your bandages come off for good."

Morgan sat straight and still, feeling as if her limbs had turned to stone. When she could see again. Except there was no Trent to see.

"What do you mean they haven't told her?" Liza was incredulous. She'd stopped by Max's shop to see Roth.

Roth shook his head. "Nope. Haven't said a word about him dying. Nutso, huh?"

Liza blew air through her closed lips. "Cruel too." She felt genuinely sympathetic toward Morgan. "You think they'll tell her soon?"

"They'll have to."

"Will you tell her if they don't?"

Roth glanced up from his chore of sterilizing Max's inking equipment. "No way." He hadn't shared with Liza his witnessing of Morgan's bizarre behavior under the old tree from the day before. Remembering gave him shivers. "I think today's the day she's supposed to get her bandages off for good," he said.

"They should say something about Trent before then," Liza said sagely. "She shouldn't be thinking he's going to be waiting for her." Yet even as Liza spoke, it dawned on her that without Trent around, Roth would have a clear path to Morgan. Why had it taken until now for her to get it? Jealousy crept up her back. She added, "Morgan will probably never get over Trent. That happens sometimes, you know. Love that never dies."

Roth felt a tightening across his shoulders. He wished he hadn't said anything to Liza. He'd forgotten how much Liza disliked Morgan. He laid the sterilized tools out on a clean towel.

"You want to do something tonight?" Liza asked casually.

"Like what?"

All she wanted was to be with him. With him, near him, close to him, in his arms, kissing him. That hadn't happened in so long that she could hardly remember the last time. *How do you make somebody want you the same way you want him?* she wondered. "Movie? I have a few bucks saved." She didn't want him to think it was a real date, just a way to hang, so if she paid her own way maybe he'd go.

"I promised Carla I'd help her wrap presents tonight."

"For who?"

"Some charity. She does it every year, then drops the gifts off at some shelter. I'd better stick with the plan."

"Maybe I could help and we could go to a late show," Liza suggested hopefully.

Roth hunched over the clean equipment and began to sort it into groupings. "Some other time," he told her without meeting her gaze. "Maybe after Christmas."

Bitterness swelled in Liza. Roth was putting her off, rejecting her. He couldn't see what was right in front of his face—Liza loved him desperately. Morgan may have been the one with bandaged eyes, but when it came to Liza, Roth was the one who was blind.

Morgan sat in Dr. Harvey's exam chair as he cut through the bandages around her eyes. Paige sat close by. Morgan could hear her deep breathing. The doctor said, "The room's darkened, Morgan. Your eyes will have to adjust to light gradually, so keep them closed until I tell you to open them."

Morgan's heart was pumping hard, boosted by adrenaline and tension. Her world had been dark for so long. She'd learned to navigate without vision, had fallen back on her other senses, discovered them enhanced in ways even she hadn't expected. Her hearing was sharper, more acute. Smells had depth and direction as never before. Her sense of touch was amazingly honed, textures seeming to come alive beneath her fingertips. Even her sense of taste was better developed. Still, she longed to see the world again. She craved color and intensity to flood her senses and bring brightness back into her life.

And yet, no amount of sight would bring back Trent. Adjusting to that loss was depleting her, drying her up from the inside out. Without him, would the world ever be colorful again? Without his smile or his touch—even his imaginary touch—would she ever be the same?

The last of the gauze fell away. Morgan felt the cool air on skin that had been covered for so long.

"I'm lifting the plastic shields," Dr. Harvey said. "Keep your eyes closed, though. You should open them gradually."

Although the soft shields and bandages weighed little, Morgan felt as if weights had fallen off her face. The freedom felt delicious. She heard Paige stifle a sob of emotion.

Dr. Harvey touched his gloved thumb to one eyelid. "Feel that?"

"Yes."

"Good." He touched the other closed eyelid. "Your eyes are going to feel as if they've been glued shut, so lifting those eyelids may be sticky at first."

Dr. Harvey dipped cotton pads into sterile water and smoothed them over Morgan's eyes, explaining every step as he went along. "Don't be alarmed if you only see shapes at first. Everything will be fuzzy, but your vision will clear and brighten over the next few days. That's why you must wear sunglasses for a while."

"I have them," Paige said.

Morgan heard her mother fumble with something in

her purse. Morgan's heart continued its wild thundering thud in her chest.

"All right," Dr. Harvey said. "Let's open those pretty eyes of yours."

Morgan urged her lids to lift. When they obeyed, she sat wide-eyed, staring into the room.

"So what can you see?" Paige asked.

"There should be a little bit of light," Dr. Harvey said.

Morgan turned her head to the right, to the left. She brought her head back to center position. "Well, you're wrong, Dr. Harvey. Everything's black. I can't see a thing."

23

Kelli felt as if her tears would never dry up. She was sick and tired of crying, and yet she couldn't stop moving from one tear-filled crisis to another: the unwanted pregnancy; Mark's abandonment of her; the explosion at school that had killed friends and teachers, made her miscarry and damaged Mark, putting him permanently in a wheelchair; and now the news that Morgan couldn't see, not even after her eyes had "healed," and extensive testing could find no reason as to why she was still blind. "No physiological reason," Morgan's doctors had said. Which left only one place to go. Her blindness was in her head, locked inside her mind.

Worst for Kelli was that her mother, Jane, didn't seem to get it. "I understand that you're sad, Kelli," Jane would say. "But life goes on. You can't grieve forever."

Why not? Kelli wondered. Grief was familiar. She knew

the ins and outs of it. Jane took her to one of several grief counselors the school had chosen; with classes to begin again in mid-January, visiting with a counselor was mandatory for all survivors of the atrium, and available to the other students. Kelli was told she had post-traumatic stress disorder—PTSD. *No kidding.* Kelli found the session unsatisfactory. How could she bare her soul to this stranger? She came home with pamphlets on grief management that Jane pinned on the kitchen bulletin board and that Kelli ignored.

Her most difficult task was visiting Mark when he came home from a physical rehab center. His mother greeted Kelli at the front door, her manner tentative but kind. "Mark's in the sunroom." She led Kelli to the back of the house. The screened sunroom had been transformed into an all-season room with real walls, hardwood floors, furniture and all kinds of rehab equipment. Mark was in a wheelchair doing arm exercises on a cable machine. He stopped cold when Kelli and his mother entered. His face reddened. Kelli knew he didn't want her seeing him like this—his physique gaunt, his once-powerful football legs already shrunken with atrophied muscles. Instant pity swelled up inside her.

"I won't stay long," Kelli said, both for Mark's and his mother's benefit. His mother left and an awkward silence descended. Kelli broke it first. "You look good."

Mark shook his head. "Why'd you come? To gloat?"

"Because I care." She wasn't his enemy. How could he think she was glad he was crippled?

He eyed her skeptically but said, "I'm going to walk again. You wait and see."

She had no idea what his doctors had told him about his paralysis, but she knew Mark well enough to know he had set his own goal in spite of whatever he'd been told. "That's good. I figured you'd go for it."

His expression softened as he accepted her assessment. "No football, though. Not ever."

He turned his head so that she couldn't see his eyes, but she suspected tears. He'd loved football. More than her, more than their baby. She asked, "Will you come to school when it reopens? Will you graduate with our class?"

"Not sure. No rush to graduate. No more coaches waiting in the wings to offer me scholarships. My folks said they'll hire tutors if I want them."

Jane had given Kelli no such option. "I'm going back."

"How about Morgan? She returning?"

Kelli shrugged. "You hear that she's still blind?"

"I read it on the Edison site. I heard her docs can't explain why." Blogs by Edison students were all over the Internet and social networking websites. Everyone had something to say, some gossip to spread. Most of it was speculation or untrue, but not the news about Morgan's eyesight—that was all true.

"She has to go to a shrink because she should be able to see," Kelli said before she thought. "Um—that's not for publication. She told me but doesn't want it to get spread around yet."

"I can keep a secret."

She recalled how carefully they had both kept their secret. Of course, it didn't matter now. A wave of grief crashed through her. "I should go," Kelli said, clearing her throat. "I just stopped by for a minute."

"Tell her hi for me, okay?"

"Next time I see her."

"I miss Trent. You're lucky that your best friend is still alive."

That much was true. "So are we, Mark."

He held her gaze for a long time and she could tell he didn't feel lucky to be living.

His despondence made her terribly sad. "I—I should go."

"Glad you came by," he said.

She didn't believe him. She left the room quickly because she didn't want to break down in front of him. Kelli had made it to the front door when Mark's mother stepped into the foyer and put her hand on Kelli's hand before she could turn the doorknob and rush outside. "I—I want to say something," she said.

Kelli didn't turn; she simply braced for what she might say.

"Our first grandchild . . . we wanted him. We would have loved him with all our hearts. You and Mark would have always had our support and help, no matter what." Her voice broke. "Would you have kept him—the baby?"

Chills went through Kelli as the words soaked into her. "I would have kept him." She almost added the word "alone," but checked herself. No need to confess that Mark hadn't wanted their grandson. There was too much pain already. She eased open the door, stepped out into cold bracing air that stung her face and numbed her nose and cheeks.

She got into Jane's car, turned on the engine and heater, shivered until the heat filled the interior. She thought of summer days from the year before. Days of soaring happiness when nothing mattered but being with Mark and when their love had been all-consuming. She could have told his mother the truth. She could have wept and railed and seethed about her hurt and his rejection. Yet she hadn't. It had been an act of kindness, of thinking about someone else's feelings more than her own. Who knew kindness had been lurking in her heart? "Good going, Kelli," she said above the sound of the auto's heater. "You're a fine Big Girl. You have been kind to Mark and his mother. Maybe you can be kinder to yourself now."

Morgan was sent to a psychiatrist, a doctor who was more than a counselor, because her soul was scarred so deeply that she needed special treatment—behavioral therapy and perhaps medication. People didn't remain blind for no reason.

The shrink, Dr. Wehrenburg, was a kind middle-aged woman with a quiet voice and a way of making a panicked patient feel calm in her presence. And Morgan and her parents needed calming. Without a medical reason for her continued blindness, Morgan speculated that she was going mad. Dr. Peg, as she liked to be called, insisted this wasn't the case after a few sessions. "You've suffered a severe trauma. This is post-traumatic stress, survivor syndrome and, I believe, conversion disorder, which was once called hysterical blindness."

"Meaning?" her mother asked.

"Morgan saw something so traumatic that her mind is unable to cope with it."

"I saw my school blow up. Wasn't that traumatic enough?"

"No one else is blind," Paige countered over Morgan's statement.

"You may have seen something else," Dr. Peg said to Morgan directly. "Something your brain doesn't want to relive."

"I 'saw' my dead boyfriend," she said bitterly. "He talked to me. Hugged me."

"A coping mechanism," Dr. Peg said. "There may be something else, though."

"How am I supposed to know what I saw if I can't remember it?" Morgan snapped at the doctor.

"That's where I come in—to guide you, help you." Dr. Peg's voice was soothing, but not patronizing.

"How?"

"Talking about your trauma with me. Talking in a group with other PTSD patients. Perhaps another event or conversation will trigger the memory. I believe you'll eventually remember, and when you do, your sight will return. You have a lot going for you—a supportive family, intelligence, determination."

"How long? I'm a senior. I want to go to college. I don't want to be blind!" But even as Morgan said the words, she felt as if she were stepping through mud, pulling and tugging on sludge inside her head that wouldn't move.

"We'll get this dealt with, Morgan. Don't give up."

Later, on the ride home, her father said, "You're going to whip this, honey. You'll go to college. Even if we have to hire a tutor for you while you attend."

"Won't that be fun. Me and my red-tipped cane and a tutor taking notes for me." Morgan gripped the armrest in the car's backseat, needing something tangible to hold on to. "School starts up next week. I wanted to go back."

"If that's what you want—"

"I don't want everyone feeling sorry for me!" she cried. "I'm the student council president, not a pity party waiting to happen."

"Everyone's hurting," Hal said. "The whole school. The whole community. Everyone's scarred. Go back or stay home. This is your call."

Morgan heard her mother say, "There's someone in our driveway."

As the car rolled to a halt, Paige said, "It's Roth." She opened her car door. "Roth?"

Morgan heard him approach, stamping his feet against the cold that was now rushing inside the auto and stinging her face.

"I—I'm sorry to just show up. I tried your office and your cell, but couldn't get hold of you."

"It's all right. What's happened?"

Morgan heard her mother's attorney voice kick into gear.

"The cops called. They want me down at the station now. They want to interview me about the explosion."

24

"Thank you for coming in, Mr. Rothman," Detective Sanchez said, stepping inside the interrogation room.

Roth's nerves were in a tangle. The detective and her partner, Wolcheski, had kept him and Paige waiting for more than twenty minutes in a small windowless room once they'd arrived at the station. The walls were a dirty cream color and marked with smudges and scrapes. The table was chipped and scarred, the chairs straight and uncomfortable. Everything about the room was shabby government issue.

"Standard procedure," Paige had told him after ten minutes with the detectives a no-show. "They want you to sweat."

"It's working," Roth said.

Max had tried to go in with Roth and Paige, insisting, "I'm his legal guardian."

Sanchez had stopped him. "Sorry. Your nephew is eighteen. No longer a minor. You'll wait out here."

Carla had squeezed Roth's hand hard. "We'll be here to take you home."

By the time the detectives came into the stuffy room, Roth was ready to jump out of his skin. They took their places, Sanchez sitting across from Roth and Paige, Wolcheski standing by the door. "Can I get you anything?" Sanchez asked. "Soda? Water?"

"A quick interview," Paige said, sounding irritated. "My client came of his own accord."

Sanchez opened a file folder. "I see you have a list of complaints for bad behavior."

"No charges, though," Paige said.

Sanchez ignored her. "Truancy—multiple times. Graffiti on school walls. Fighting on school property. One school suspension. A complaint of petty theft."

"Charges dropped by the store manager," Paige said.

Roth relaxed a little. His lawyer didn't act the least bit perturbed. He was ashamed. A few years of toeing the line weren't going to make up for his previous bad behavior in the cops' eyes. Once bad, always bad, he surmised. No room for his life's circumstances.

Sanchez looked up, offered a tight smile. "You have tats." She said it as if it were a character flaw.

Roth glanced down at his arm, at the ink band of barbed wire circling his right wrist. He tugged down the sleeve of his sweatshirt. "My uncle's in the business. My tats are free. And I like them."

"I don't think body ink is against the law, Detective," Paige inserted.

Sanchez shut the folder, leaned forward. "Well, I'll tell you what is against the law, Mr. Rothman. Setting off fireworks on school property and having the school evacuated."

Roth felt his heart seize and sweat beads break out on his forehead. How did they—? He sidled a glance at Paige, certain that she was going to get up and walk out of the room because he hadn't told her about his September prank.

To her credit, Paige leaned toward the detective, cool and collected. "And you can prove this?"

"We read the Edison blogs and social network pages, Mr. Rothman. You've been ratted out."

"Hearsay," Paige interjected. "Those sites are filled with conjectures and rumors. Kids love to trash-talk and you can't separate truth from fiction."

Sanchez eased back into her chair. "But it leads me to ask a most important question. Wouldn't fireworks be one step down from setting an actual bomb? A test run, so to speak?"

"Are you asking? Or charging?" Paige wanted to know.

"I want to know if your client set that bomb that killed nine people," Sanchez said bluntly, not taking her eyes off Roth. "And I want him to answer."

Shaken, Roth said clearly, "I did not set off any bomb."

"Please remember, my client ran into the school to help victims," Paige said quickly, her voice rising in pitch. "He saved several lives by his quick actions."

"Including your daughter's," Sanchez said, looking squarely at Paige for the first time since they'd all sat down.

Paige ignored the comment. "Are you charging my client with anything?"

Sanchez waited a couple of beats before speaking. "Not at this time. But we reserve the right to recall him for questioning. And so will the FBI."

Paige stood and Roth scrambled up beside her. Wolcheski stepped aside at the door, but not before giving Roth a suspicious stare. Roth's heart banged hard inside his chest. The cops thought he was guilty. And he couldn't prove that he wasn't.

"Don't leave town," Sanchez threw at their backs.

"My client will be in school," Paige said over her shoulder. "He plans to graduate with the rest of his class, so of course he'll be staying."

They stepped into the corridor. Roth's shirt was soaked with sweat that had bled through to his sweatshirt. "I—I'm sorry—" he started.

Paige shushed him, walked him out to where Max and Carla were waiting. She held up her hand to stop them from approaching just yet. "You should have told me about the fireworks," she told Roth

"I—I know. I was stupid. I should have told you. I should never have set them off in the first place. That was stupid too." He raised his head, looked into her eyes. "You acted like you knew about it. In—in there . . . in the room."

"I read the social networking sites too, Roth. Of course I know the gossip."

He felt his face redden. "I did the fireworks. But I never set a bomb. I swear to God."

She shook her head in disgust with his confession. Still, she said, "I believe you. I would never have agreed to defend you if I didn't believe you. Plus, Morgan told me you would never do something like that."

"Sh-she did?"

"My daughter's a good judge of character, and I trust her judgment. Now go home. And go back to school when it starts. Tread carefully. Stay out of trouble. We're on your side."

Executioner was nervous. Apocalypse had come over, shut them up in Executioner's bedroom and gone to work posting messages on several social networking sites from Executioner's computer. "Finished," Apocalypse said, signing off the latest posting. "If this doesn't lead a trail straight to Stuart Rothman, nothing will. The cops are dying to charge someone."

"It—it's real anonymous, isn't it?"

"And encrypted. Do you doubt me?"

"No! Never! I just want to make sure it can't lead back to me . . . us," Executioner added at the last second. Apocalypse was scary, but Executioner wanted to send the message that they were in this together.

Apocalypse swiveled the office chair and stared coldly at Executioner. "Don't ever doubt me. I don't like my motives being called into question. You agreed with my plan. You are as guilty as I am. But I don't expect to get caught."

Executioner swallowed hard. "I just want to be careful." Licking dry lips, Executioner asked, "Is it true? Did Roth set the fireworks?"

"I heard rumors. Why do you think I hatched this plan to do him one better? Roth's a creep. A stupid creep. Thinks he's badass with his tats and piercings. Our school's hotshots thought they were more special than the rest of us, but we showed them. We took the bunch of them down. We're superior. Especially that Trent and Mark. I really hated them."

Executioner did a throat clearing, hair standing up on both arms. Apocalypse was reveling in intellectual superiority, with not an iota of fear. Executioner was genuinely scared. "The—uh—rumor is that the queen bee is still blind."

"Yeah," Apocalypse said with a mirthless laugh. "Ain't it sad? Green eyes, now dark, too bad. Hey—I'm a poet."

Executioner laughed, not because the rhyme was funny, but because laughter was expected. The "poetry" had been delivered coldly, with absolute cruelty and without remorse. Apocalypse looked at Executioner and added, "I'm the best there is when it comes to sweet revenge."

25

Liza's heart almost stopped when she opened her front door and saw Roth on her doorstep. He hadn't come over in months, and when he did show up, she looked awful, having fallen asleep on the sofa watching television. "Roth. You should have called." She pushed her hand through her ragged hair.

"Can I come in?"

"Sure, sure." She backed away. "Want to sit? How about a soda?"

"This isn't a social call, Liza." He didn't follow her out of the foyer.

She came back to stand in front of him and saw that his expression was anything but friendly. "So why are you here?"

"I spent the afternoon at police headquarters being questioned."

"No way."

"They think I set the bomb, Liza."

The news rattled her. "But why? Why you?"

His face went stony; his eyes glinted. "Someone wrote about me setting fireworks off last fall. It's all over the school blogs."

She was still a little dulled from being awakened from a sound sleep, but slowly realization crept over her. "Are you accusing me of writing the blog entries? Because if you are—"

"I'm just stating facts. Some writers have hidden their identities, so I have no idea who posted the info. The cowards. I just know I confided in you about what I did. You blabbed then. Now it's back, all over the Internet. The cops even read it."

Her face went hot and her stomach queasy. "I would never do that to you."

"I haven't forgotten. You already did last fall when you mentioned it to your friends."

"I doubt they even remember after all that's happened now."

"Then why am I being dissed? Why is my name all over the place as the likely school bomber? Have you read these postings lately?"

"No," she said coolly, trying to regain her equilibrium. "My computer's been down for weeks and Dad says we don't have the money to get it fixed right now."

Roth slammed his fist into the wall, making her jump. He cursed and scowled. "You were the only one I told!"

"Morgan figured it out," Liza said angrily. "Why are you blaming me? Maybe she said something to someone."

Roth looked at her incredulously. "You saying *blind* Morgan posted the blogs? That's low, Liza."

Liza squared her chin, backpedaled. "I'm just saying maybe others figured it out like she did."

Roth shook his head, glared at her in disgust. "Stay away from Morgan, Liza. And when school starts next week, stay far away from me too."

"Get out of my house," she hissed, furious at his accusation and attitude.

"I'm gone." Roth yanked open the door and retreated into the falling snow. Liza slammed the door so hard behind him that the upper window rattled. Heartbroken, she felt like crying.

"Damn you!" Liza screamed. But there was no one to hear her. Her misery crystallized into a searing pain that made her drop to her knees and gag. Her wrath smoldered, burned itself out like a fire without oxygen, and was swallowed into the silence of the house. Roth hated her. He would go to Morgan now and she would take him. Liza was sure of this. School would start and Liza was condemned to see Roth and Morgan together everywhere she turned.

Liza was out of the picture with Roth. What she didn't know was what she was going to do about it.

The entire Grandville community was invited to tour the new atrium the weekend before classes were to begin. The students had lost more than two months of class work—three weeks of which would have been Thanksgiving, Christmas and New Year breaks. The remaining weeks were to be made up by early June. The school board had voted to forgo spring break, and by extending classes one hour each day, the year could be finished, exams given, and diplomas handed out on time. There was little opposition to the plan. People just wanted the terrible year over.

"Tell me how it looks." Morgan was with her mother in the crowded atrium, aware on some level that people were staring at them, but determined to ignore stares and whispers and finish the year with her class. She'd been ambivalent for a few days, but in the end knew she wasn't a quitter regardless of the odds. Blind or not, with or without Trent, she was going to complete high school. She wasn't going to throw away twelve years of hard work.

"It's been redesigned," Paige said. "The staircase is solid. No more cantilevering. That design was left over from the seventies anyway. The area looks contemporary, clean and fresh. Brighter too. One wall is painted royal blue and stretches two stories. The skylight is back, bigger, though."

"And the wall?" Morgan thought of the place where students had congregated, and where so many lives had been lost.

"Gone. There's a memorial pedestal with a large bronze plaque. And with, um—" Paige stopped.

"The names of those killed," Morgan finished matter-of-factly. "What else could they put there?" She held on to her mother's elbow as people brushed past. She felt the heat of their bodies. "Show me," she said. "I want to touch his name."

Morgan smoothed her hands, almost as useful as her eyes after weeks of blindness, over the contours of the memorial. She formed an image of its shape in her mind, found the cool flat surface of the bronze's slanted front and felt the raised letters one by one. "Mr. Simmons," she said after a moment. She read off the names, for she had memorized them all by now. "'Trent Caparella' . . ." Tears clogged her throat. She'd sworn to herself that she wouldn't cry in public. A broken vow.

"You look good," Roth whispered into her ear.

She turned toward him, surprised because she hadn't felt him come alongside of her. "Oh, hi."

Paige said, "Place looks pretty good, doesn't it?"

"Brand-new," Roth said.

"Who's here?" Morgan asked Roth.

"Media, and tons of kids, parents, some police."

"Police?"

"Crowd watchers. Guess they don't want anything to spoil the grand unveiling."

Morgan heard a bitter undertone in his voice. She knew that he'd been questioned and she felt sorry for him. He'd only helped people. The real bombers were still out there, maybe even here today. For a moment fear tingled up her back.

Roth clasped Morgan's hand in his. "Can I take over the tour?" he asked her mother.

"Mom? Would you mind?" Morgan asked.

"Fine," Paige said. "I see the mayor and I want to talk to him."

Roth's hand felt warm in hers, and she wished she could see him. Crazy how his presence could light up her day.

"How have you been?"

"All right," she said. "Going to therapy. Hasn't helped yet."

"But you're returning to school?"

"I am. I'm the president, you know." She gave a wry smile. "Met with the new principal, Mrs. Mecham, on Friday. She's nice and knows about tragedy: she lost two sons in the Iraq War."

They kept walking, and Morgan realized they had left the atrium and were going down a hallway, because the noise grew dimmer. Roth stopped. "Know where you are?"

Morgan turned her head slowly, sniffed the air. "Lockers by the smell of it."

He laughed. "Very good. You're standing in front of your locker."

She reached out, put the flat of her palm on the cold hard metal. Her fingers bounced the combination lock. A new realization dawned. "I—I won't be able to see to open it."

"I'm sure they'll let you lock it any way you want to.

And . . ." Roth paused, then added, "I'll be your eyes whenever you want. I mean, if you want me to be."

Tears threatened her again. What had she been thinking, that she could return to school? She was stupid! Returning totally blind was impossible.

"Hey, hey." Roth cupped her face in his hands. "You can do this. People will help. I'll help . . . your friends . . . Kelli, all of us will help."

She nodded, not trusting her voice. There were no guarantees her sight would return, and the line between dependency and helplessness was a balancing act. Morgan needed to distinguish between them if she was going to live inside of darkness, perhaps for a long, long time.

26

Mrs. Mecham started Monday morning with a rally in the school gym, calling it a "new day" and a "fresh start." Morgan sat in a chair beside the new principal in the center of the gym. She heard the rustle of feet, the subdued voices of kids in the bleachers. No one was whistling or yelling or calling out to others. This was a somber time and everyone sensed it. Cameras clicked away around them, but the school board had banned television crews from the gym—only digital cameras were allowed. Cell phones had been confiscated for the event. "A private gathering that I won't let be exploited," Mrs. Mecham had said.

Mrs. Mecham spoke about the victims as honorable, made some uplifting remarks, then turned to Morgan and offered the microphone to her. Morgan stood, amid hushed whispers. Her heart was thudding and her mouth was cotton dry, but still she stood, shook out her red-tipped cane and tapped it on the floor. "Trust me," she said. "Anyone gets out of line, I know how to use this."

Her levity allowed everyone to laugh, which broke the tension. She heard cameras click. She continued. "We all feel the holes left by the faculty and students we lost. Not only the ones who died but also the ones who left Edison because of what happened. We are what's left." She took a breath. "Good for us."

A couple of shouts of approval burst from the bleachers.

"So that means we're in this together. We're going to finish this school year. Seniors will graduate. The rest of you will move on to the next class level. It's going to happen."

More positive cheers came from the bleachers.

"I know I'm blind. But I'm still your class president. I will stay this year. I will finish my term and my studies. The bomb may have flattened our atrium, but it won't flatten my resolve." Her heart beat even harder and her voice rose. "I will not be broken," she said loudly. *"We will not be broken."* She said each word with volume and deliberation. She raised the mike into the air and shouted, "Not broken!"

The chant started instantly, swelled into a triumphant shout as hundreds of voices joined in, followed by foot stomping and wild applause. Morgan's throat swelled with emotion and tears filled her eyes. Edison would not be broken.

. . .

Morgan's speech was a rousing success. Afterward, when Roth was walking her to her class, with her holding his elbow, he said, "Great speech. In fact, I felt something stir up inside of me when everyone started cheering."

"School spirit?" she said.

"Indigestion, probably." She pinched him hard. "Ow!"

"Don't mess with me, mister."

He laughed and so did she, a feeling of elation filling her.

But if school was shaking out in her favor, her therapy sessions weren't. Dr. Peg worked with her every week, but she could get no nearer to the source of the trigger that had rendered her blind. Together she and Dr. Peg revisited Morgan's memories of the days before and the day of the explosion. Morgan strained to recall every detail, because remembering the sequence of events was the key to unlocking her mind.

"You saw something terrible, something that shut you down," Dr. Peg told her, coaxing Morgan to pull out every detail inside her head for examination.

Morgan "saw" images, flashes of scenes, from the fateful day. She felt Trent holding her close to keep her warm, the softness of his down-filled jacket against her cheek, even smelled the nylon fabric. She remembered glancing over his shoulder and seeing a backpack under the staircase. The FBI had found scraps of the backpack and the time-sensitive detonator that had been used in the bomb. She remembered being curious about the abandoned backpack, and the flash of bright light as it exploded. She remembered everything except the one thing that held the key to her eyesight.

"It may be a series of things," Dr. Peg said. "Your sight may return gradually or suddenly. The more we expose your memories, the more likely we are of success."

For Morgan, "exposing memories" brought on horrific headaches that often incapacitated her for the rest of a day or evening. But she continued her therapy because she didn't want to be blind for the rest of her life.

She had plenty of help at school too. Roth had been right about that. Different seniors took on the task of walking her from class to class, getting her seated and her recorder set correctly. Roth drove her to and from school every day, and Kelli helped Morgan navigate the cafeteria at lunch. Mark did not return to Edison, choosing instead to attend a small private school. Kelli told Morgan, "He can't face coming back. The wheelchair and all. I mean, he was a star once."

"It would be hard for him," Morgan said.

"I miss him . . . you know, the old Mark. I think he should have stayed at Edison. Kids would have been nice to him. We stayed."

Morgan clasped Kelli's arm, a show of understanding and friendship. "Dr. Peg says we all handle bad things differently. Look at me—my brain shut down my vision. Do you ever go visit him?"

"Not anymore. It hurts us both too much. Best to move on. I've a lot to push out of my mind. For me, the situation is a mixed blessing in some ways."

Morgan heard the sadness in Kelli's voice and ached with her over her losses. The girls never talked about the pregnancy.

"Do you think whoever planted that bomb will ever be caught?" Kelli asked.

"God, I hope so. Hard to think someone could walk away scot-free."

"But it wasn't Roth? Like the blogs are saying?"

"It wasn't Roth."

Kelli sighed. "He likes you, you know."

"Maybe. I think we're just all wound up together. His case, Mom defending him, him pulling me from the rubble, and now feeling like he should help me in some way," Morgan mused. "Mixed up together. Like lines blurring together."

"I see the way he looks at you," Kelli said, confident of her analysis. "His eyes follow you everywhere."

Morgan tried to dismiss Kelli's words, but all that came to her was a long-ago night in the moonlight when Roth had undone her hair. Another life. "I need to get to class," Morgan said, rising from her cafeteria chair. "Are you my Seeing Eye dog?"

"Woof-woof," Kelli said, and held out her arm to her friend.

They hadn't been in school three weeks when Mrs. Mecham dismissed classes early due to an approaching blizzard. Roth turned into Morgan's driveway in near whiteout conditions, got them both inside. "Stay," she said. "It's too dangerous for you to drive. I hear the wind howling."

Her house was empty and he really didn't want to leave her alone. "You sure?"

"Mom and Dad are in Grand Rapids and I'll bet they're stuck too."

In the kitchen, she pulled out her cell phone, called her mother. "I'm home," she said.

"Good. The highway patrol just shut down the roads, so we'll have to wait until the storm's past. I hate for you to be by yourself."

"A friend's with me."

"That's a relief. You and Kelli take care of each other."

Morgan didn't bother to correct Paige's assumption. "Will do."

"Keep in touch as long as you can," Paige said, but the cell service was already breaking up. Morgan flipped her phone closed.

"Whoops," Roth said. "We just lost power. It's going to get pretty cold in here." He was glad to be staying, eager to be near her as long as possible.

"Not a problem," Morgan said. "Help me gather some food and let's go to the den. We have a fireplace and a gas log you can start with a butane lighter."

Within twenty minutes, Roth had built them a fortress on the floor from sofa pillows and blankets, and Morgan had stocked it with bread, peanut butter, fruit, crackers and bags of chips. The fire was glowing and heating the room nicely. "Caveman digs," he told Morgan, snuggling her into the nest.

"I want my bed pillow. And Bingo. And my iPod."

He brought all three from upstairs. "Really cold up there."

She stretched out on her tummy, her face to the fireplace, savoring the warmth on her skin. "We have candles in the kitchen. I can't see, but you may not like sitting with me in the dark."

"Fire's good enough," he said. His fingers itched to touch her, but she seemed oblivious to his nearness.

She wasn't. She wished she understood her attraction to him. At the beginning of autumn, when he'd hardly been on her radar and she'd gradually grown aware of his covert looks in her direction, she'd been wary and unsettled. He had a reputation for trouble, but perversely, as time went on, she liked having him rake her over with his surly but sexy gaze. Later, when she got to know him, she discovered he wasn't like his reputation. He was rough-edged, moody and guarded, decorated with body art, but also thoughtful and caring, and undeniably sexy and attractive to her. And now they were alone together. She told herself to be careful.

"Peanut butter cracker?" he asked.

"Not yet." She turned on her iPod. "Good until the battery charge dies," she said as music floated into the room.

They talked for a while, the force of the wind rattling windows now and then. The grandfather clock in the foyer chimed six times. Roth was amazed at how quickly the time had passed with her. "You seem to be making a good comeback," he said.

"I act better than I feel. I'm really scared, you know."

"I don't believe it. Morgan Frierson isn't scared of anything."

"You have more faith in me than I do."

He gave up the battle to keep his hands off of her and reached over and smoothed a tendril of hair off her face. Her eyes were wide, unseeing, reflecting the firelight. The den was quiet except for soft music and the snap of the fire. "I get what it's like to be scared," he said.

Her skin trembled at his touch. "Now I don't believe you. You could have been killed going into the school to help us."

"Knee-jerk reaction. I had overdue library books. Didn't want to face any fines."

She giggled. "Most people would be afraid of explosions. Everyone else ran."

"I've seen explosions before," he said, without meaning to say it.

"What do you mean?"

The story of his orphaning spilled out of him, haltingly at first, then more quickly as he told her what it was like to watch his parents die. "I was locked in the car, but I could feel the heat through the window. The fire melted the paint on the outside of the car. No one should die that way."

Morgan was stunned by his story, left speechless as the

images came alive in her imagination. For her the pictures were like a horrific Hollywood movie; for him they were terrifyingly real. Her heart hurt for him, for the helpless little boy seeing a holocaust destroy his parents. She turned herself onto her back, put up her hand and touched his face.

"Hey," he said, catching her hand in his. "You're not going to get all soggy on me, are you? All that happened years ago."

She ignored his words. "You were so young. What happened to you after . . . after they died?"

"Foster homes. Two were all right, one not so much. Max eventually got me when he got out of the service. Rough going until Carla came along. She holds everything together."

Roth's life had been so different from Morgan's, and she saw the differences plain as day. She didn't need Dr. Peg to help her understand why Roth had been in trouble so much, or why he wore his "bad boy" image like a shield. He felt safe behind it.

He said, "And so now what I have to deal with are the police and the FBI. What lousy luck."

"Who else knows your story?"

He thought about it. Liza, because they'd been friends since sixth grade, and, of course, "the system" that had shuffled him around like an unwanted object. "I keep it to myself. There's hardly anyone I've told."

She lay quietly, listening to Roth's breathing. She could tell he was leaning over her, his face very close to hers.

Her breath quickened. Warmth from the fire and blankets made her feel languid and soft. Fearful of her own emotions at the moment, she sat up.

He swung his leg over her lap so that he was balancing on his knees. He cupped her face between his hands. "May I kiss you?"

She froze like a statue, her heart a pounding runaway train. No one had ever asked permission before. Thinking about it, she realized that she'd never kissed anyone except Trent. Her memory of him rose like a ghost. And yet . . . and yet . . . "Yes." The word slid out like the single note of a song. She wanted him to hold her. She wanted Roth's mouth on hers more than anything.

His kiss came softly, his lips full and tender, pressing hers and exploring the shape and contours of her mouth. His kiss was different from Trent's. Trent had held her tightly, pressed her mouth harder, often urgently, as if he wanted to consume her. Trent had made her sizzle. Roth made her melt. His tongue explored hers and she felt as though they would fuse into a single being. His hands remained on her face. She arched toward him, craving to have his body lean into hers.

He pulled away, touched his forehead to hers. She was certain her skin would burn him, but instead he only sucked in deep breaths and ran his thumbs along her cheeks.

Roth was shaken by the kiss. Perhaps because he'd waited for so long before tasting it. Morgan was the girl he'd wanted for years, and yet he felt no triumph in the moment. All the kiss had done was make him want her more.

"We have a whole night ahead of us, Roth," she whispered, suddenly frightened. She had managed to damp down the flames she'd felt when she'd been with Trent. They'd set limits such as never being alone together for too long. They'd reveled in touching and tasting and heavy petting, always stopping short of abandonment. With Roth, Morgan knew it was different. She wasn't sure she could control what was happening inside her with him. Her longings when they were with each other were different. Need, not curiosity, drove her. And now, alone and without barriers . . . Her teeth chattered and she began to tremble.

Roth caught the scent of her fear and steadied himself. Maybe it was too soon. Maybe she was thinking of, and comparing him to, Trent. He didn't want that. He lowered her onto the pillows, leaned down and kissed her closed eyes. "I'll take whatever you want to give me," he said. "Nothing more."

She wanted to give him all of herself. She was lonely and sad and confused, all at the same time. And burning with need. "I . . . don't . . . know. . . ."

He pressed his fingertips to her lips. "It's all right. It's okay." He knew what he wanted, but he wouldn't push her. "This is for you to decide," he said reluctantly.

At that moment, his will was all that stood between them.

She turned onto her side. "Hold me."

He wrapped his arms around her and snuggled against the curve of her body. He stroked her hair until she stopped trembling, and he stared into the dark until her breathing became even and regular in sleep.

27

The FBI showed up at the Rothman residence two days after the storm with search warrants for the house and for Max's place of business. Max called Paige and then headed down to his shop, where Hal was waiting for him. Carla stayed behind with Roth. The search was methodical and thorough. Nothing in the house or garage was left undisturbed. When Paige arrived, Roth asked, "Can they do this? They're tearing the place apart!"

"They have legal warrants," Paige said grimly. "Ignore them."

Roth sat between Paige and Carla on the sofa, the two women protecting him like iron walls. Inwardly he did a slow burn, bouncing between anger and fright with every drawer opened, every shelf's contents put on the floor. "This sucks."

Carla patted his arm. "Hey, hey, be careful," she called

to one man. "That vase is valuable. Came all the way from China."

The man gave her a quizzical look. Roth snickered. There was nothing of great value in the house. Most things had come from local secondhand stores.

"Where's your computer?" one of the men asked Roth.

Roth looked to Paige and she signaled he could answer. "I don't have a computer."

"What do you use for Web surfing? For homework?"

"I use my uncle's, at his shop."

The man went back to trashing the room, then moved on to the bedrooms.

"How did they get the warrants?" Roth asked. "I didn't do anything."

"The blog chatter and your interview by the police. And because they have no other suspects," Paige answered. "They're desperate."

Morgan struggled to keep her sanity and her good grades afloat in spite of being blind. She recorded class lectures, listened and relistened to her teachers' words. She took verbal tests, aced most of them. But inner turmoil over her lost sight, along with her vanished sense of control, sneaked out to haunt her when she least expected it. Her emotions were up, down, like a roller-coaster ride with no end in sight.

She ran student council meetings, was astounded by the kids who suddenly wanted to be a part of the group. "Nothing like an explosion to pump up school spirit," she told Roth one afternoon after he ushered her inside her house.

"I can't recommend it as a game plan," Roth said dryly.

"Mom? Dad?"

"No one here but us."

They'd gone into the kitchen. "You want something to eat or drink?"

"Can't stay. Promised Max I'd help around the studio." His strategy for self-control when near Morgan was to not spend too much time alone with her—difficult, but necessary.

She was disappointed. She liked hanging with him. His company kept loneliness at bay.

Roth said, "Oh, here's your mail. Picked it up off the floor when we came in."

Her interest pricked up. "Is there anything for me?"

He thumbed through the short stack. "Coupon for free fish sticks."

"I'll pass."

"A letter for you from Boston College," he said, turning the envelope over in his hand. It looked pretty official.

Her breath caught. "Open it and read it to me. Please."

She listened to the tearing of paper, the unfolding of a letter. He read, " 'Dear Morgan—' " He stopped.

"What does it say? Tell me what it says." She was as jumpy as a puppy.

"It says you've been accepted into their fall freshman class."

She squealed. "Oh my gosh! This was my first choice!"

Roth stood reeling as the implications hit him. "You're going away to college?"

"That's always been my plan. I want to go to law school someday. I want to have a great job and travel and . . . oh, you know, all that stuff."

"But what about—"

"Blind people go to college," she interrupted. "I can't let it stop me."

He felt petty for bringing it up. Her blindness was never supposed to hold her back, but he hadn't thought beyond the end of high school. She would leave and he couldn't follow.

She fumbled in her purse, which she'd set on the countertop, for her cell phone. "I've got to call Mom and Dad. Oh my gosh!"

Roth felt pressure in his chest. He didn't want her to leave. He wanted her to stay. He wanted her with him. He heard her reach her mother and excitedly tell her the news. Roth retreated from the room and walked out the front door, locking it behind him.

Roth lay on his bed in the dark. He'd kept the lights off because the darkness matched his mood. Morgan had dreams and plans. He did not. He had no plans in place after graduation.

There came a gentle rap on his bedroom door. *Go away.* The door cracked open and Carla peeked inside. "Can I come in?"

He said nothing, but she entered anyway. Carla eased

down beside him. Roth threw his arm over his eyes to block out the stream of light from the hall that cut a line across his chest and stopped below his chin.

"You missed supper."

"Yeah. I wasn't hungry."

"You should eat something."

"I'll have a bowl of cereal later."

Carla sat quietly for a few minutes. "What's got you down?"

"Oh, I don't know. Maybe because I'm the chief suspect in my school's bombing."

"You're innocent and we all know it," she said. "And I don't think that's all that's eating at you."

"Carla, please . . ."

"It's a girl, isn't it?"

"Why would you think that?"

"Guys don't give up food unless they're having problems with love."

"I'm not in love," he said, but he didn't sound convincing even to his own ears.

"It's that girl you told me about last fall, isn't it?" Carla's voice was soft, kind and sure. "The one you wanted to go after."

Roth was amazed how quickly his stepmother had zeroed in on the truth. True, he couldn't get Morgan off his mind. "How do you remember a little conversation we had months ago?"

"I care about you," Carla said as if that explained everything.

Silence descended. Roth heard the movement of his clock from across the room, the muffled sound of the TV from the living room, where Max was watching a basketball game. Roth wanted to be alone but didn't know how to kindly make Carla go away.

"Do you know what was the worst day of my life?" she asked suddenly.

He sighed.

"It was the day my doctor told me that I could never have a baby of my own."

Roth turned his head so that he could see her face. Light haloed her silhouette—the frothy hair, the slope of her shoulders. "Sorry," he mumbled.

"Do you know what was the best day of my life?" She let the sentence hang for a heartbeat. "It was the day I moved in with you and Max. I got two kids at the same time." He heard the smile in her voice. She flipped Roth's hair off his forehead. "You are a great kid, Stuart."

He cringed at the use of his given name but was still moved by her compliment. "Your point?"

"That's my point. You're a great kid and I love you. Somewhere out there in your future life there's a girl for you. A lucky girl. You may not recognize her at first when she comes along, but be on the lookout, because she'll appear when you least expect her."

He wanted only Morgan.

"Now come on," Carla said, tugging at his elbow.

He didn't want to leave the dark, but he let her lead him into the kitchen and fix him a sandwich anyway.

• • •

Morgan called him on a Saturday morning. "I need you to come over right now."

Alarmed, Roth asked, "Is something wrong?"

"No. Something's right. Big-time right."

He raced over in his blue pickup in record time, on freshly plowed roads, his heart pounding. Her voice had been upbeat and excited. Maybe she'd gotten her eyesight back. He'd known it might come quickly when it came. And if she could see, what would it be like between them?

Morgan threw open the front door the second he stepped on the porch. She threw herself into his arms, hugged him tightly. "It's over," she said, her eyes glowing but still sightless. "They've caught the kids who made the bomb!"

28

"Over?" Roth repeated. Had he heard correctly? "Is that true?"

Over Morgan's shoulder he saw Paige walk into the foyer. She beamed him a smile. "It's true. Morgan wanted to be the one to tell you, but they've caught the bombers."

"How? Who?"

"Come into the den and I'll tell you everything," Paige said, motioning Roth forward.

Roth hadn't been inside the den since the night of the blizzard when he and Morgan had tenderly touched and explored one another until they finally fell asleep in each other's arms. He kept his eyes on Paige, looking for any sign that she knew about that night, but saw no hint of it as he and Morgan settled on the sofa. Paige took a place in an easy chair beside the fireplace.

"First, 'who,'" Paige said. "Do you know a Tommy Watkins or a Jackson Sinclaire?"

Roth came up blank. "No. Should I?"

"They're ninth graders," Morgan threw in. "I don't know them either."

"They did the deed," Paige said.

Roth's jaw dropped. "But why?"

"Let me tell you what I know," Paige said, leaning forward in her chair. "I was in police headquarters last evening with a client and the place was buzzing about two kids who'd been brought in earlier and were sitting in separate interrogation rooms. Cops do that, you know. They separate suspects and then question them to see how their stories match up."

Roth remembered his own interrogation and how accusatory it had been. These guys were no doubt treated the same way.

"FBI showed up, so I knew something important was happening. I hung around the precinct eavesdropping. Turns out these two boys were in the hot seat. Of course, their parents were with them, and attorneys from Detroit, but the cops were pretty sure they'd got their bombers. I overheard Sanchez talking—you remember her."

Roth would never forget the woman. She'd been like a bulldog with him.

"Sanchez is saying that one kid, Tommy, cracked like an egg the second the cops pressured him—confessed to everything, cried like a baby. His lawyer couldn't get him to shut up. But the other one, Jackson, he was cold as ice.

Clammed up at first, but when he heard his friend had confessed, and he knew it was over, acted proud of what they'd done. Didn't seem to care a whit about murdering teachers and fellow students."

"*Ninth* graders? At Edison?"

"'Fraid so."

"But why?"

"According to what I overheard, when an agent asked that question, Jackson answered, 'Because I could. Because I felt like it. I was nothing to them. They were nothing to me.' The agent tried to give him an out. He asked him, 'Were you bullied? Is that why?' 'Bullied?' says Jackson. 'Naw . . . I just told you, they don't even know we're alive.'"

Morgan stirred beside Roth on the couch. "We don't have cliques at Edison . . . do we?" She aimed her question at Roth.

Morgan and her crowd had been part of Edison's elite, top of the high school pecking order. How could Morgan not know this? "I'm not the one to ask."

His answer stung her—she felt she'd worked hard to make everyone feel involved with the school.

Seeing Morgan's reaction, Paige said, "Life is cliquish. People tend to hang out with others like themselves. Groups form. It's human nature. Perhaps no one could have made these two feel like they fit in."

"So now what?" Roth asked, not wanting to be sidetracked.

"I marched up to Sanchez and asked if this confession

vindicated my client. She said it did, so you're free to be the hero we know you are." Paige looked smug and satisfied.

Roth didn't feel like a hero. He felt used and abused. Neither could he get his head around how two kids could cause so much damage and affect so many lives when they seemed to have no grudge against anyone. Why would anyone commit such a detestable random act of violence? There was no logic. "I still have a lot of questions," he said.

"We all do," Paige answered. "And trust me, this story will be pounded to death by the media over the next few weeks. Some things we'll learn, some things we'll never know. They're in the courts' hands now. Your involvement, it's over."

Paige predicted correctly. The minute the story broke, the media was all over it. The national media returned to Grandville like flies to a carcass. The local reports were far more sensitive, because those media outlets shared in the town's grief. The two boys were charged as adults, and their names made public. Interviews were extracted from anyone who'd stand still in front of a microphone. Reports soon labeled both boys as "young minds gone awry, smart and from decent homes" with "ordinary families." Roth learned that while both their sets of parents worked, Jackson and Tommy had unlimited free time and access to almost anything they wanted. He wondered how he might have turned out if his parents had lived and he'd been given an "ordinary life." Of course, his parents would have had to give up drugs. He wouldn't think about that.

The FBI had the best forensic science people in the world and they found traces of explosives in Jackson's garage five months after the bomb had been assembled there. They traced the backpack to Tommy from a fifth-grade photo, and they broke the encrypted code of both boys' computers to find a trail of incriminating emails and blog entries to throw suspicion on a Stuart Rothman, a senior at Edison. For his part, Roth refused all interviews, wanting only to put it all behind him. He hated that the two creeps were being immortalized, even as monsters, by the media.

Carla read the newspaper stories aloud daily at the breakfast table. "Makes my blood boil," she said. "These kids are monsters. A psychiatrist is calling Jackson a sociopath. That's a person without a conscience." Fuming, she looked across the table at Roth and Max. "Are you two listening?"

Max shoveled a forkful of scrambled eggs into his mouth. "Let it go, *ma chérie.*"

She squinted at him. "These two almost wrecked Roth's life. How can I let it go?" She returned to reading aloud. " 'The suspects referred to one another as Apocalypse and Executioner in their emails.' What jerks!"

"Please, Carla, I'm sick of the whole mess," Roth said. He concentrated on the back of a cereal box, hoping to discourage Carla's rant. Roth had precious few months to go before June graduation and he was working double-time to make sure it happened for him. Although as a fringe benefit, his "not guilty" status had cut him some slack in his classes. None of his teachers wanted to flunk a hero.

Carla shook out the paper, ignored Max's and Roth's wishes. "'Police and FBI acted on an anonymous tip before issuing warrants for Mr. Sinclaire and Mr. Watkins.'"

This part piqued Roth's interest. "What kind of tip?"

"Says it came via an email to headquarters. They traced it back to a computer at the public library—no way to know who sent it. The note said: 'In the case of the Edison bombing, you should look at Jackson Sinclaire and Tommy Watkins.'" She folded the paper and hit the table with it. "So why is this tip coming out now? If someone knew something, why didn't they report it sooner?"

"No idea," Roth said, returning to his cereal bowl. If he could get his hands on the tipster, he'd shake the answer out of the creep.

"They'll probably get off on an insanity plea," Carla grumbled.

"They won't get off," Max said. "The feds frown on bomb makers." He winked at Roth, who grinned and hunched over his cereal bowl, transfixed not by the conversation but by the Cheerios floating in milk, bobbing up and down with every dip of the spoon, but unsinkable—a metaphor for his life.

Liza stood in the crowded convenience store, hiding behind a row of metal shelves that held snack foods, and watching Morgan stand in front of the refrigerated cases of soft drinks. Liza had ducked when Morgan and Roth entered the store, not wanting to be seen by Roth. Bad timing that they were in the same place at the same time. She'd steered a wide berth around Roth since their argument weeks before. It pained Liza to see the two of them together at school, so seeing them after school twisted inside her like a knife.

Morgan reached for the handle of the glass case, but her blindness was keeping her from opening the case. Liza understood the dilemma at once.

Liza glanced to the front of the store, at the line of people waiting to pay for gasoline. Roth was a good ways back and Morgan was hidden from his line of sight. The sole cashier was swamped, so it was going to take Roth a while to get to the man with his cash.

Liza fidgeted. She knew what she *should* do. She should help Morgan.

Morgan grasped the handle of the cold case, but was stumped over how to choose a soda. She'd insisted that Roth pay for gas while she grabbed a soda, and so he'd left her to her own devices, which, at the moment, were failing her. How had she thought she could pick out a diet soda from refrigerator shelves she couldn't see? This blind thing was getting old.

She'd thought for sure that the capture of the kids who'd planted the bomb would bring her sight back. It hadn't, despite Dr. Peg's continued assurance that her conversion disorder would vanish when her mind was ready to deal with it. She gritted her teeth, determined to drink whatever she pulled out of the case even if she hated it.

"Need some help?"

The female voice sounded somewhat familiar, but Morgan couldn't place it with a face. She'd heard so many voices in the past months that were faceless. "Note to marketers," Morgan said half-jokingly, "here's an idea. Let's put talking shelves into stores to help the sightless choose a product."

"Not a bad idea," Liza said. "Do you know what you want?"

"Diet cola," Morgan answered, hating that a stranger had to wait on her. She should be used to dependency on others by now, but she wasn't. A rush of cold air hit her face when the girl opened the door. "I'm Morgan," she said. "Who can I thank for helping me?"

"A fellow student," Liza said, unwilling to say her name, and hoping Morgan wouldn't recognize her voice. They hadn't spoken since that day in their junior year when Morgan had been campaigning for the class presidency. In truth, she didn't hate Morgan Frierson. The girl had paid too big a price in the explosion, and over the several months that Morgan had championed the school and its students, Liza had formed a grudging respect for her.

The thing between them was Roth. Liza was pretty sure that Morgan didn't even know this, plus it wasn't as if Morgan had snatched Roth away from Liza. It really wasn't Morgan's fault that Roth wanted her instead of Liza, she tried telling herself. She glanced at the line at the front of the store, saw that Roth was getting close to the register. He was flipping through a magazine and not watching Morgan like a hawk. "Can you make it to the front of the store?"

"Sure," Morgan said, shaking out her red-tipped rod. "I'm a trained professional."

Liza steeled herself against a wave of sympathy. Instead a twinge of jealousy flared inside her. She couldn't help it. She couldn't shove it down.

Morgan held out her hand. "The soda?"

"Oh, sure." Liza held the can for a lingering moment, then perversely shook it before handing it over. She regretted it as soon as Morgan took the can and started up the aisle, moving her stick from side to side.

"Let me buy it for you," Liza called, trying to turn the tide of her action.

"Thanks, but I've got the money. I appreciate your help."

Liza almost ran after her and grabbed the can out of her hand, but a quick glance forward showed her that Roth was next in line and he'd turned to watch Morgan coming toward him.

Liza stepped behind the safety of the shelves, hiding her body and her shame from Roth's blue eyes.

29

Outside in the car Roth asked, "You have any trouble finding the soda you wanted?"

"I didn't find it. Some girl from school was back there and she dug it out for me."

"I would have helped you," Roth said.

"I'm sick of people having to help me," Morgan snapped. "I'm sick of everything!" She tossed her purse onto the floor beside her feet.

He stuck the key into the ignition, letting her vent because he knew she hadn't deserved what had happened to her. "Want me to open the can?" he asked patiently.

"I think I can handle a pop-top," she groused, and slid her forefinger under the ring of the top, jerking it backward in one angry motion.

Soda exploded from the can, spewing foam upward, into Morgan's face, and across the front of her sweater. In an instant two things happened. Violent missing images fell into place inside her head. And blinding light pierced her darkness.

Morgan screamed.

She asks, "What's that?"

Trent turns his head to look over his shoulder.

A flash of white light erupts, followed by the sound of a boom.

Trent pushes her away from him so quickly she crashes backward onto the tile floor of the atrium, hitting her head so hard she sees stars.

Breathless, she watches Trent's down-filled jacket burst open and white fluff balloon into the air. Trent's blood sprays down on her in a mist of fine red rain, and the world goes black.

The images took only microseconds, but Morgan saw them all as clearly as she was now seeing the sunlight gleaming through the windshield of Roth's car. She covered her eyes with her hands and began to rock and cry.

Her eyesight had returned in a cloudburst of memories that her brain had sought to repress for months. Her eyesight had returned with the terrible vision of watching her beloved Trent die.

Morgan looked up at the tree in her front yard, at a web of branches beginning to burst with new green leaves. Soon the leaves would canopy the branches and shelter the trunk and the ground beneath, where she stood. She hadn't ventured to the tree in months, not since the winter day she'd learned Trent was dead.

The spring air was chilly, but the snow was mostly gone. Daffodils and a few brave tulips pushed up from flower beds in front of her house. Waves of sadness rolled over her heart as she remembered all the times she and Trent had stood beneath the tree and clung to each other. The image of Trent's blood spraying down on her may have returned her sight, but it had not quelled her sense of horror and loss. His body had taken the impact of the explosion, and his quick action had saved her life.

"You okay?" Roth asked. He'd walked out to the tree with her, his hands jammed into the pocket of his familiar black hoodie. For some reason this tree had special meaning in her life. He felt like an intruder.

Morgan couldn't tell him the truth about her and Trent and the tree. It wouldn't be fair. "Just wishing spring would hurry up and get here," she said.

She'd returned from a checkup to find Roth waiting for her on the porch.

"Your checkup go all right?"

"Eyes are fine. But I'll stay with Dr. Peg through the summer. She says my PTSD needs some TLC before I head off to college. She wants me to go away strong."

"You're still going?" He knew the answer, but needed to hear her say it.

"Absolutely I'm going. I was going to go when I was blind. Of course, now that I can see, it will be better."

Roth scuffed the toe of his boot against a lump of hard

earth. "Can I ask you something?" He didn't wait for her answer; he just forged ahead. "If Trent was alive, would you still go?"

Roth rarely weighed his words, but she understood why he wanted to know. "It was always the plan between us. Trent would go off to college and so would I." She shrugged. "That's the truth."

"But you took his promise ring. What was that all about?"

She had locked the ring in her jewelry box when her eyesight returned. "I'm not sure. It was going to be hard for both of us to let go, but I think we both knew college would change us. The ring was a way to hold on to the past. Not always the right thing."

Roth got her unspoken message—he also would soon be in her past. He released a lungful of trapped air, rocked by what he knew was happening between them, the inevitability of their goodbye.

"What about you?" she asked. "What will you do in the fall?"

"Work with Max. He wants to bring me into his business in a big way."

"College?"

"Not now. Maybe someday." He couldn't face the idea of more studying just yet. He would graduate by the skin of his teeth.

"Speaking of Max," Morgan said, "can I ask a favor from you?"

He peeled a chip of bark from the tree's trunk, searching inside himself for a way to let go of her. "What is it?"

She told him.

He raised his hands, backed away. "Whoa! You sure about that?"

"Way sure."

"Your mother will kill me."

"I'll handle my parents. I know what I want. It's really just a matter of timing with them. Last minute's usually best."

"I'll talk to Max." Roth knew he should go. Dragging out their breakup wasn't going to help either of them. "Guess I should roll. I told Carla I'd help clean out the garage." He turned and walked toward his pickup.

She watched him go, her heart hammering. It couldn't end like this between them. She loved him, would always love him. He had saved her too, and not just because he'd pulled her out of the ruins before the stairs fell. Throughout the months of her blindness, he'd been with her, beside her. "Wait." From under the shadow of the tree, Morgan ran after him, threw her arms around him.

His arms flew around her and he buried his face in her long red hair.

"I won't be leaving until August. Can't we be with each other until then?" Staying together for the next few months was only postponing their parting, but it was what she wanted. She was unsure of what he'd do. Roth could very well walk off, and she wouldn't blame him. He owed her nothing.

"That what you want?"

"More than anything."

He felt like a prisoner given a reprieve. He wanted any

part of her he could have, for any length of time he could have it. "Convince me."

She turned her mouth to his. "Just shut up and kiss me."

He did.

30

Edison High School's senior class is proud to announce
the graduation celebration ceremony of
the Class of 2014,
on Saturday, June 14,
at the Grandville Civic Center,
419 Center Street, at two o'clock in the afternoon.
The town of Grandville is invited to attend.

Morgan's announcement read:

Mr. and Mrs. Halston Frierson, Esqs.
announce that their daughter, Morgan Marie Frierson,
will graduate with honors from Edison High School
on June 14, 2014.
She will continue her education
at Boston College in the fall.

Roth's, at Carla's insistence, read:

MAXWELL AND CARLA ROTHMAN
ARE DELIGHTED TO ANNOUNCE
THE GRADUATION OF THEIR SON,
STUART "ROTH" ROTHMAN,
FROM EDISON HIGH SCHOOL
ON JUNE 14, 2014.

Roth had wanted to add "against all odds and the better judgment of the faculty," but Max and Carla had nixed the suggested wording with laughs. "I never doubted you'd graduate," Carla told him.

Max and Roth just looked at each other. Both of them certainly had.

In a powder-blue sky, the June sun drenched the day with warmth as the civic center filled up. Inside, dignitaries, government officials, media, parents, friends and family watched as 105 graduates in royal-blue caps and gowns made the march down the aisles and onto the stage. Names were called one by one to receive diplomas. Nine empty chairs sat at the front of the stage under a spotlight, in memoriam, for the people who were lost forever and could not celebrate this day.

After the ceremony Roth stood with Morgan and Kelli, their arms hooked together for countless photos by their families out on the lawn. A giant white tent graced the lawn, where tables overflowed with refreshments. No graduating class had been treated so royally. Grandville was still a small town, but this class was special. They were the survivors, the ones who had endured and triumphed over a tragedy nobody could quite comprehend.

Roth couldn't stop grinning, especially when he looked at Morgan. Her beautiful green eyes sparkled in the glow of the sun, and she glanced toward him at every chance.

"Over here! Look at me," Jane called.

The trio turned to face her camera. "How's your mom doing?" Morgan asked Kelli from the corner of her mouth.

Kelli tipped her head, grinned big for her mother's camera and whispered, "I think she's finally growing up."

"Really?"

"She isn't dragging me down her high school memory lane anymore."

"You must be so proud!" Morgan teased.

"I am," Kelli said, putting her hand over her heart. "All grown up at thirty-seven. I'm going to miss my little girl."

Morgan erupted into laughter.

"What's so funny?" Roth asked. He was still holding a half-eaten cupcake thick with blue icing that he'd picked up at the refreshment stand earlier.

"You!" Kelli said, and pointed. "Have you looked in a mirror?"

He glanced between Kelli and Morgan. "Why?"

"Your lips are blue," Morgan said.

"And your teeth," Kelli added.

"Ewww," both girls said in unison.

"Then have a bite," he said, swiping each girl's mouth with the gooey blue frosting.

They shrieked but ran into the tent for a cupcake of their own.

"Are you absolutely positive you want to do this?" Max asked Morgan, who sat in front of him in his studio.

"Why do you and Roth keep asking me that? I know what I want." She shot Roth an exasperated look.

"I'm just saying it's permanent," Roth told her.

"A tattoo can be lasered off," Max explained. "But it's expensive and painful. Roth and I are just making sure you realize what you're about to do."

Morgan nodded fiercely. "I get it. I want it. Now let's do it."

Max asked, "You eighteen?"

"Since April."

He nodded. "The first pass will scab over and heal, then you'll need a touch-up after a couple of weeks."

"The U-Haul leaves in three. So we need to start today."

Max limped to his bookshelves, pulled off several books, brought them to her. "Pick out a design and tell me where you want me to place it. Wording too."

"I want it here, on the inside of my forearm, because I want to see it every day of my life. And I already know what I want it to say." She waited for several seconds as a lump of emotion closed off her throat. Getting herself under control, she said, "I want two names only—Roth and Trent, inside a beautiful heart."

Roth's gaze flew to her face. "My name?"

"You both saved me from dying."

He searched her eyes, saw her determination, grinned. "Who gets top billing?"

She laughed. "Why, you do, of course."

Max readied his tattoo needles and pots of ink while Morgan and Roth pored over the books for just the right heart for her to wear for the rest of her life.

Epilogue

LIZA STOOD AT THE PLATE-GLASS WINDOW of Main Street Café, where she worked, watching the sparse flow of two o'clock traffic. She untied her apron as she waited, her work shift over for another day. She'd been waiting tables at the small eatery since six that morning, as she'd done six days a week ever since graduation. The work was interesting and the regulars friendly. Plus she needed the job.

Outside, the November day was gray and a few stubborn leaves clung to trees in the chilly wind. Almost a year had passed since the school bomb had altered so many lives. The accused bombers were still awaiting trial—the wheels of justice ground slowly. She'd be glad when the "anniversary" was over—the local media were featuring stories already, and the city council was planning some sort of memorial ceremony on the actual date. Kids most affected and traumatized had been contacted and quoted.

Morgan's mother had interceded for her daughter with "Morgan is away and happy at college." Liza heard that she'd added, "Do not contact her about that horrible day, or you'll have our law firm to deal with." Scuttlebutt from café patrons had Morgan staying gone this first Thanksgiving after the bombing. Liza hoped so.

When a reporter had ambushed Kelli in a parking lot at the community college, Kelli had shoved the mike away and snapped, "Why would I want to talk about that day? Please leave me alone."

On-air reports noted that Mark, formerly one of the best football players in the state, had been sent to a top rehab center known for its successes with paralyzed war vets. He would never play ball again, but he might be able to walk after the center's rigorous and groundbreaking therapy.

Roth's interview as the "hero" had been peppered with too much profanity to be put on the air. He'd ended by saying, "Don't you guys get it? We all want to forget the bombing, not remember it."

As for Liza, she had been across the street from the school that day, so she was not on anyone's radar.

She had reinvented herself too. Her hair had grown out and the bizarre purple spikes were now little more than fading tips in the dark brown mass of curls. Most of her studs were gone too. Only two remained in her ears and one small silver sphere glittered from the side of her nose. The tats that showed on her arm she kept covered with concealing cream. Her hair almost covered the one on the back of her neck, and clothing covered the ones on her left shoulder and across the small of her back. She still loved her body ink but had realized in June that it was time to move forward with her life. That meant looking less like a sideshow, more like the rest of humanity. Individuality came from the inside, not from an outside layer of applications.

She had her own place now, a studio apartment over Mr. Anderson's garage two streets away—close enough to walk to work. She was saving for a car. She'd used all her graduation gift money for the apartment—first and last months' rent and a hundred-dollar damage fee. The place was small, with a pullout sofa at one end and a tiny kitchen area at the other. Her mother had helped her hang curtains and paint the walls. Liza wasn't sure if it had been a gesture of love, or of eagerness for her to move out.

"You still here?" Gracie asked, coming out of the kitchen balancing plates of food for the only two customers in the café. She was four years older than Liza, divorced with a three-year-old daughter, but had become Liza's best friend. Gracie handled the afternoon and supper crowd. They worked Saturday nights together, often going out for fun after closing up the place at nine if Gracie could get a sitter. Not much to do in Grandville, but it was home.

"I'm going," Liza said.

"Waiting for that blue pickup to pass?" Gracie asked knowingly.

Liza colored, but kept her face toward the window. "Nosy."

"You going to do anything about it today? You've been watching it drive by for five months and never done a thing about chasing it down."

"These things take time." In truth, she was scared to reestablish contact with Roth. She still wanted him more than anything, but she was afraid he might reject her once more. On graduation day, out on the lawn of the civic center, he'd come up to Liza while Morgan was in the refreshment tent, wrapped his arms around her and given her a bear hug. "Sorry," he whispered in her ear. "I acted like a jerk to you and I shouldn't have. We still friends?"

"Not a problem," she told him, basking in the warmth of his embrace. "Lot of pressure on you back then."

He'd grinned, kissed the tip of her nose and gone inside the tent.

She'd run into him only once more, in the summer, when they'd both been pumping gas at the convenience store. He was two pumps over when she'd pulled in, without noticing him at first. He'd called her name and waved, a genuine smile on his face. Her heart almost beat out of her chest at that moment. She'd silently pleaded for him to walk over, but he didn't. He jammed the gas cap onto his truck, waved, shouted, "Got to run! Catch you later." Later hadn't come.

They'd been friends since sixth grade and Liza had seen him grow from a hostile, broken little boy into a defiant wild adolescent and, ultimately, into a pretty stable guy. She'd watched from the fringes of his life for a solid year, and now hoped he might see her in a new light—Liza, the girl who loved him.

She saw the blue pickup turn the corner, and stepped back from the window. Her gaze followed it down four blocks, where it parked in front of the Ink Spot. She watched Roth hurry inside.

"Go on," Gracie said, "or I'll drag you down there myself. I've been thinking about getting a tat. What do you think?"

"You'd faint at the sight of the needles." Liza grabbed her coat. Gracie was right. If she was going to go down there and face Roth, she should go ahead and do it. She struggled into her coat.

"Call me, however it turns out, good or bad," Gracie said, before the door closed behind Liza.

Outside, Liza took deep breaths of the cold air to steady her nerves. Her case of nerves was more than just trying to get together with Roth again. Other things troubled her. Liza had secrets—two that she'd sworn to herself she'd never tell anyone. First, she'd been the person who'd shaken the cola can, causing it to spurt foam in Morgan's face. Even though it had been the event that had washed away Morgan's blindness, it had also slammed Morgan with horrible and disturbing memories no one should have to confront. Liza was truly sorry about the escapade. She knew that Morgan was out of Roth's life because she was off at college. It was weird to know that in some ways she'd saved Morgan, because her sight came back, but also got rid of her, so maybe Roth would now need his old friend back. Her guilt . . . her secret to keep.

She wanted a cigarette, then remembered she'd quit smoking three months before. She turned north on Main Street, toward Max's shop, clutched her coat to her throat as a chill dove down her blouse. She was going to have to remember to bring a wool scarf tomorrow.

There was another secret. That one she would also take to her grave. If she told anyone, she'd find herself in the center of a maelstrom. Or perhaps retribution. Her fear of both was real. Liza had been the tipster who'd vindicated Roth, the one who'd sent the anonymous email to the police from the library's public computer. She had shifted police and FBI interest to the two ninth graders after learning their names and tracking them at school for weeks, covertly watching their actions and cocky "I've got a secret" attitude. She had been the one who'd seen them pacing outside the school on the day of the bombing. She'd not considered it at the time, but in hindsight, she recalled their looks of glee when the atrium exploded. She'd seen them exchange high fives with each other when the front of the school erupted with screams and smoke and sounds of falling rubble and with kids swarming out of the building, scrambling for their lives. She'd been too shocked and traumatized herself to remember much except the exodus. And her heart had been in her throat when she watched Roth rush into the building to help.

It had taken months for her to recall the details of that terrible day. Although she vaguely remembered mentioning that she'd seen two boys to Roth, her brain still hadn't put their behavior into sequence. But when blogs and accusatory words showed up on websites that focused police attention onto the boy she loved, Liza's memories fell into place completely. If they'd never put the blame on Roth, Liza might never have remembered their actions and self-satisfied smirks while Edison was falling down. She might not have put it together.

Liza's stroll had brought her to the front door of the Ink Spot, and now her heart was going crazy. She still had an opportunity to turn and retreat. She prayed for courage. This was it. The big moment. Would Roth welcome her? Would he be polite but standoffish? Would he be indifferent? She fixed a bright smile on her face, took a few more deep breaths. It was amazing what a girl would do for love.

Liza opened the door.

About the Author

Lurlene McDaniel began writing inspirational novels about teenagers facing life-altering situations when her son was diagnosed with juvenile diabetes. "I saw firsthand how chronic illness affects every aspect of a person's life," she has said. "I want kids to know that while people don't get to choose what life gives to them, they do get to choose how they respond."

Lurlene McDaniel's novels are hard-hitting and realistic, but also leave readers with inspiration and hope. Her books have received acclaim from readers, teachers, parents, and reviewers. Her bestselling novels include *Don't Die, My Love; Till Death Do Us Part; Hit and Run; Telling Christina Goodbye; True Love: Three Novels;* and *The End of Forever.*

Lurlene McDaniel lives in Chattanooga, Tennessee.